Her Boss's Baby

Lexie Miers

Chapter One

"Mr. Martinez is waiting for you Miss Louis," the beautifully dressed woman addressed Sarah with a polite smile and gestured for her to follow.

Sarah pushed herself out of the firm leather chair she occupied and followed the woman in the sexy black suit. She envied the confidence it took to wear a suit that was tailored so beautifully. It covered her knees and cleavage, but it highlighted every curve the woman had. She didn't have a good enough body to get away with wearing anything that tight. If this woman was any indication of the women Enrique Martinez hired, Sarah's Australian size fourteen bottom would not do!

"Good luck," the beautiful woman said as she headed back to her desk.

Inhaling a deep breath, she pushed open the heavy wooden door with as much courage as she could muster. She had been dreading this interview for weeks.

"Miss Louis, please have a seat."

A dangerously sexy and lightly accented voice reached her from the far end of the room. It belonged to a man who had his back to her while he stood, searching through a filing cabinet.

"Thank you, Mr. Martinez," Sarah replied as calmly as she could, forcing her unsteady legs to propel her forward.

Silently congratulating herself on making it thus far, Sarah sat in the seat opposite his desk.

When her potential employer turned around and sat facing her, Sarah's heart leaped in her chest. She had read once that your pupils dilated during physical attraction and for the first time in her life, she wished there was a mirror at hand so that she could check.

Enrique Martinez had jet black hair that matched his even darker eyes, olive skin that bespoke his bloodlines, and a square jaw line. Why had no one told her that the infamous Spanish tycoon had a face that looked like angels had designed it? Why hadn't she found a photo of him before the interview? She may have been more prepared!

"Miss Louis, why did you apply for this position?"

Sharp and fast, the direct first question broke through the haze of physical attraction like a sharp knife through bread.

"Well, I..."

Where was her greeting? Where was the question as to her wellbeing?

"Miss Louis if you cannot answer a simple question, I doubt you will be able to instruct my niece in the English language."

Sarah's mouth dropped open. He'd just insulted her. Her spine stiffened. She had almost perfect scores in English in her graduating year at University, and he was insinuating that she couldn't hold a conversation? Well, beauty certainly was only skin deep after all!

"Then allow me to answer the question more succinctly, Mr. Martinez." Sarah lifted her nose in the air.

She wanted to walk out when she saw the corners of his mouth lift in a goading smile, but instead she clenched her hands into fists and let his arrogance strengthen her resolve.

"I applied for this position because the timing was perfect. Also, because I was interested in moving to a country I had never lived in before. My previous charge, whom I have been with for three years, has begun school and her parents have chosen to take a more active role in her life."

Sarah's chest tightened with each word she spoke. How dare he insult her?

"Why would living in Spain interest you?" Enrique asked her, leaning back in his chair, studying her.

He flicked his eyes over her, and Sarah's anger rose in her belly.

"I have never been to Spain, but some of my best friends have. They all tell me it is one of the most beautiful places in the world. I don't speak Spanish. However, your advertisement said it wasn't necessary."

"Do you believe you are right for this position Miss Louis?"

Sarah looked him straight in the eye. "Yes." She had no doubts.

Enrique studied her for a moment before asking, "Why?"

He lifted one eyebrow up in the air, and Sarah's temper melted like an ice block in a hot house. He was too attractive for her sanity.

"I believe my references speak for themselves, Mr. Martinez," Sarah repeated with another uplift of her chin.

Enrique gestured for her to continue.

She let out a small sigh and gave into his silent request.

"I have worked with three separate children as their full-time nanny. They were all your niece's age. I specialized in the preschool years in my studies and found myself to be excellent at interacting with that age child. You can ring anyone of my previous employers, and they will give me a reference."

"We already have Miss Louis; that is why you are here. The people I spoke to said that you enhanced the life of their child. However, what I want you to tell me is why you are unique enough to be hired for this role?"

She inhaled sharply, why did his rudeness keep surprising her?

"I am not going to list off my qualities to you, Mr. Martinez. My resume was obviously enough to get me this interview. I am not a vain person and find it insulting that you would ask me to sell myself to you by listing virtues with no proof as to their truth. If you have a specific question, ask away."

Sarah loved the shock she saw written in Enrique's wide brown eyes. So glad, in fact, she thought she just might do a jig on the table.

Sarah kept her eyes fixed on the man in front of her. No way was she going to be intimidated. Even if he was the most good-looking man she had ever laid eyes on. He would have to be six foot three inches tall, with shoulders as broad as a footballers. Why was he giving her such a hard time? Could she handle living with a man whose eyes made her stomach quiver, but whose rudeness made her want to smack him like a 5-year-old child?

That last thought brought a smile to her lips. Smacking him, now wouldn't that be fun?

"What's amusing, Miss Louis?" Enrique snapped.

"Am I not allowed to smile, Mr. Martinez?" Sarah asked sweetly, feeling powerful and a little giddy.

"Of course, you are."

Sarah waited for her prospective employer to get his temper under control and waited for him to continue. She wasn't apologizing for anything.

"How do you discipline the children you look after Miss Louis?"

"It depends on what they have done wrong." Sarah chewed on her lower lip, trying to remember the times she had disciplined her charges. They weren't many once she established a good rapport.

"Most of the time I give them a time-out or take something from them that they care about. Although positive reinforcement for only good behavior often works better. It depends on the child. I have never physically disciplined a child. I have found that if you learn what that child likes, you can use it to your advantage. Have there been problems, Mr. Martinez?"

He coughed and avoided her gaze while he shifted in his chair.

"My niece may only be three years old, but since her parents' death a month ago, she had become more and more disobedient. Throwing tantrums and screaming as loud and as often as she can."

Sarah nodded, that was not uncommon in most three-year-olds, let alone ones who had experienced such a trauma.

"I have been taking care of three-year-olds for a long time; I'm sure Amalia and I will get along fine."

She smiled to reassure him, the man that she was beginning to see as not only a potential employer but a worried uncle and new guardian.

"That is all I need to know. Are there any questions you have about me?"

"Yes, I do, Mr. Martinez. I would like to know how I will be treated. Will I be sent to live in a guest house at the other end of your property or will I live in the main part of the house? Will I eat with you or with the kitchen staff? Will I have one or two days off a week? Will I travel with you if you take your niece? Are you away from home a lot? Generally, what am I to expect from working for you?"

She watched his eyes widen, and he cleared his throat, again.

"Miss Louis, I have to be honest with you, I really can't answer many of those questions right now. My sister died a month ago, leaving her daughter in my care. I have never hired a nanny and know little of what is expected. You tell me what works best for you and we'll go from there."

He looked a little sheepish, and Sarah found herself drawn into his jet–black eyes as they opened enough for her to see a glimpse of self-doubt and, was that a touch of fear?

"Well…" Sarah began, thinking quickly about what she wanted. "I would prefer to live in the main house somewhere away from your main bedroom but close to your niece, if that is possible. I am happy to work six days and only have one day off, with the proviso that I can take more time off if needed. I tend to like to eat with my charge, wherever that is. As far as travel goes, I will go wherever your niece is. If you want her with you, we will accompany you. If not, I will look after her at home. She will be my priority; I can promise you that."

Sarah gave Enrique her sunniest of smiles. Her prospective employer shifted in his chair and looked away.

Well, that didn't go quite as planned.

He opened the top drawer of his desk and pulled out a contract, then laid it out in front of her.

"Miss Louis, if you have no other questions, you are hired. I have a contract here for you to read. You may take it home and bring it back signed next week."

Pardon? She had the job? After bullying her through the weirdest interview she had ever had, the man was hiring her? Standing up and extending her hand, Sarah decided it was time to leave before he changed his mind.

"Thank you, Mr. Martinez, I will."

His hand touched hers, and her center melted. The attraction she had been trying to deny since she had seen him flared to life. Fire licked up her thighs and centered between her legs, her core throbbing with an awareness entirely foreign to her.

She was in trouble.

Big. Trouble.

Giving him a small nod and pulling her hand from his hot grasp, Sarah turned on her heel and rushed out of his office as quickly as her legs would carry her. She may be inexperienced with men, but she knew when one was attracted to her. Could she live and work so close to this man when the attraction between them was so obvious?

Of course, you can, who are you trying to fool? He may look at you, but he probably looks at a million other girls the same way.

Sarah sternly reminded herself that she was the nanny! She was one step above a housekeeper, a servant. Sarah took a deep breath and put her life back into perspective. Enrique Martinez was a millionaire, and she was the nanny. Case closed.

Enrique watched Sarah Louis walk away, then collapsed into his chair with a thump. What had just happened?

Every other applicant had been far too happy to tell him how honest and hardworking they were. They often had un–ironed clothes and badly groomed hair. They had not impressed him with their declarations of self-worth. Instead, Sarah refused to list off her qualities, knowing that her attitude and appearance spoke for itself.

She was impeccably groomed. Blonde hair that had been brushed to glisten. Even in the strange light of his office, it was the color of sunshine. Her hair was so long it reached halfway down her back, but she had clipped it back to keep it from falling in front of her beautiful face.

Her eyes were a dark blue, fringed with long eyelashes.

She had worn mascara, lip gloss on her full pink lips, and nothing on her skin that disguised the freckles that covered her flawless, creamy complexion.

A knitted, pale blue twin set and a pair of black pants made her look young and professional, yet traditional and a little conventional. Which he liked. Especially as a role model for his niece.

Her appearance spoke volumes more than she could ever have said herself.

She was a woman with confidence in her abilities. She didn't need brand name clothing and three inches of makeup to accentuate that. She was perhaps a bit bigger than his tastes ran to, but she was perfectly proportional. Enrique found himself wondering if this was how she would always dress while working. Did she always cover herself up as was fitting for her position? Did she have a boyfriend?

Enrique stilled when he registered his last thought. Why was he even wondering about that? He'd had a very long day; perhaps it was the tiredness getting to him. He was practically hallucinating! Lusting after what his father would call 'the help.' He shook his head and got back to work.

Chapter Two

A week of utter chaos ensued, Sarah could practically see the papers and suitcases flying around her in slow motion. Saying goodbye to her family and friends was hard, but the excitement she felt in her chest every time she thought about her new adventure made up for any sadness at leaving her current home. Everything she owned was packed into two large suitcases and once again, she was rootless.

Having never worked overseas before she'd was quite flustered with the paperwork, but Mr. Martinez's secretary had taken care of the working visa.

Thankfully she'd had the forethought to have a passport organized.

She was leaving Australia, her home for the entire 26 years she had been alive. Her birthplace, her parents' birthplace. How would she fair somewhere else?

The first thing she had done after her interview was read up on her new employer. She had found out that Enrique was 35-years-old and had been born into a very wealthy family. He had inherited his father's business ten years ago, and he had remained in the headlines ever since.

Sarah knew that she could easily overcome her physical attraction to him, however, the more she read about him, the more interested she became. She admired the way he'd saved his father's company from ruin and rebuilt it to a level that surpassed the heights his father had originally made. But the way he had taken sole responsibility for his niece was the most impressive, and also the most worrying. Her heart could resist a cold, ruthless businessman. But a man who wanted the very best for his orphaned niece? Her heart may just find resisting him almost impossible.

SARAH STOOD in the international departure queue for the first time in her life, her excitement barely contained. This was the start of a new life for her, and her feet were tapping the floor like she was in a musical.

She handed her identification over to the woman behind the counter, feeling the flutter of butterfly's in her stomach once again.

"I'm sorry, you're at the wrong counter," the woman behind the desk said politely.

"Oh, I'm sorry," Sarah looked behind her, not sure what the woman meant. "I didn't realize. This is the line for the QANTAS flight to Madrid, isn't it? I just got a new job and was told to pick up my tickets. I'm sorry, I haven't flown before."

Too much information. Stop chattering.

"It's fine. You just need to line up over there," the woman pointed to the line with no one in it.

"But that's for first class passengers."

"Yes," the woman said, her tone changing to one of annoyance now. "You're listed as having a first-class ticket, so if you wouldn't mind making your way over there now, please?"

Sarah picked up her jaw and her luggage. Enrique's assistant hadn't said anything about her being in first class. Sarah handed her identification over to the beautiful woman behind the counter and had her luggage taken off her.

Woah. She did have a first-class seat.

Who had organized this for her and why? She would have been happy in economy!

Stop being so ungrateful. This is an opportunity to fly first class– something totally unattainable to you!

Sarah boarded the plane, her heart lodged firmly in her throat as she made her way to her seat. She stopped in front of the large armchair and gasped. It was huge! Her seat was the aisle seat, and as she took her very comfortable position and wiggled her butt, she wondered who'd have the window seat.

Would she have a businessman to chat with? Or perhaps a wealthy widow?

Her friends had talked about the horror of flying internationally. Cramped up in seats that only reclined inches. Never getting any sleep. As she pressed some buttons, shefound herself reclining so far back she was almost laying vertical, a giggle escaped her lips. She'd have no trouble falling asleep on this eighteen-hour flight.

She pressed the button again and sat back up. This was going to be amazing!

"Excuse me; that's my seat."

Sarah gasped as her eyes flew up to the face hovering over her. Was she hallucinating? Was she already asleep and dreaming in her super comfy seat?

"Excuse me." He repeated and awkwardly stepped around her and into his window seat.

Damn! Moving out of the way would have been nice Sarah.

"Oh, I'm sorry Mr. Martinez, I didn't expect to see you here, you shocked me."

Had she just admitted to that? Damn, that bloody honesty gene! She never could control her tongue.

Enrique smiled, though the tightness she saw around his mouth belied that there was no pleasure for him in seeing her.

"I can see that Miss Louis, however, to be honest, I am a little surprised myself. Simone didn't mention that you were on the same flight as me."

Sarah dropped her eyes to the hands she had folded in her lap.

What could she say to that? He sounded like she was the last person on the planet he wanted to see.

"Oh, it's a pleasant surprise Miss Louis, please don't misunderstand me. I, well…" Enrique coughed. "In my business, I make it a habit never to be surprised. You know, always be prepared and all that."

Sarah raised her head and laughed at his puny joke, her nervousness getting the better of her.

"Well, this is the second of two surprises for me. Simone didn't tell me I was flying first class and I lined up in the economy line."

"We always fly first class," Enrique said, his tone flat and defensive.

"Well, this is my first international flight, and I am a little nervous. Probably wouldn't have remembered my name if it wasn't written on my passport."

Sarah began pushing the buttons around her and scrolling through the movies on the TV screen in front of her.

So… cool.

"Tell me, Miss Louis, are your parents still in Australia?"

Her ribs tightened around her lungs and squeezed a little.

"Ah, no. They both passed away when I was sixteen, car accident."

"I'm sorry," her new boss mumbled. People always got uncomfortable when she told them what had happened. She didn't blame them, of course.

"Oh, it's okay," Sarah told him. It had been ten years, but it still hit a tender spot in her every time someone asked about them.

She wasn't sure if that loss would ever be anything but painful.

"To be honest, Mr. Martinez, I think that was one of the reasons I applied for this position. Being able to help a child who has gone through a similar thing… that's good for me, and her. I think."

The plane made a loud noise as it began to move towards the runway. Every flying horror story that Sarah had ever heard came flooding in. She gripped the armrests on her chair, staring at the way her knuckles showed white through her already pale skin.

Enrique reached over with one of his hands and laid it on top of one of hers. The contrast of his olive skin on hers as strange as it was surprising.

"It'll be over in a minute," Enrique chuckled.

As they reached a plateau and the plane leveled out, he withdrew his warm hand and a soft moan that escaped Sarah's mouth. She was alone again.

"It's a long flight, perhaps you too would like to sleep?"

Enrique reclined his chair and turned his head away as though to go to sleep.

Probably a good idea.

It was a long flight, and she'd be jet lagged for days if she didn't. Perhaps if she closed her eyes, she could pretend she was already there.

SARAH AWOKE FIRST, opening her eyes to see the face of an angel not even six inches away from her own. More like the devil in disguise. She smiled to herself at the thought. If the magazine articles she'd read were to be believed. His face could tempt a saint, though. His cheekbones were so high, and regal Sarah had to resist the urge to reach out and touch him. She turned her face away quickly, heat scorching her face in embarrassment.

Sarah shook herself, trying to get some perspective. This was her employer.

He was superior to her in so many ways.

He had traveled the world and slept with countless beautiful women.

Sarah got up from her seat carefully so as not to disturb Enrique and made her way to the toilet. She sat down on the seat and put her face in her hands, suddenly lonelier than words could describe.

Chapter Three

Sarah and Enrique sat in silence in the limo that had picked them up from the airport. She gazed in awe out the window at the difference in the landscape around her. Green hills and mountains. The landscape was varied and so beautiful.

Enrique typed on his laptop the entire trip. Sarah couldn't think of anything to say that would be worth interrupting him for.

They drove for more than two hours.

"We're here."

Sarah jumped as Enrique's voice broke the cove of silence around them.

"Oh, great."

Finally.

The large metal security gates swung open, and they drove for what seemed like forever along the private driveway. When the car finally pulled up in front of a house, Sarah sat transfixed for several minutes, just staring.

The house in front of her was not a mere home; it was a castle.

Enrique jumped out of the limo and strode up the stairs into the safety of his home.

His jaw ached with tightness and anger boiled in his belly like a hot soup. He hadn't got any work done on the trip from Melbourne. His computer may have been on and open for the past two hours, but he had not been able to concentrate on anything except the sound of Sarah's breathing and the sighs of wonder as they drove through the countryside of his beloved Spain.

He must keep her as far away from him as possible. She was dangerous to everything he held dear. His control, and his ability to work.

First, he had to introduce her to Amalia. Amalia, he smiled at the thought of the child. She had been her mother's reason for getting up every day and the apple of her father's eye.

At three years old, Amalia was an enigma to him. She could talk, but he couldn't have a conversation with her. Not one where he got anything out of her which was constructive.

He was grateful to finally have a full-time nanny for her.

He would find out soon enough if Sarah had been the right choice for them.

Sarah had no idea what to do. She was standing outside the biggest house she had ever seen and the only person she even slightly knew had run off from her as fast as his legs could carry him.

"You can come this way, Miss," an elderly gentleman with a very thick accent said to her.

Relief flooded her like a rushing tide.

"Oh, thank goodness you speak English, I'm Sarah," She rushed across the steps to hold her hand out to the man who had spoken to her. He looked at her hand for a moment then took it, shaking it softly.

"I'm Riccardo," the man with kind brown eyes told her, giving her a soft smile, then walking towards the stairs.

Sarah let her shoulders drop, the twist in her belly unraveling like a knotted string being pulled. A place this size would have so many staff members, she was sure to make friends.

If this man spoke English, of course, other people would, too.

"Wow!" was the first and only thing that Sarah could say when she walked into the foyer of Enrique's 'house'. Sarah followed Riccardo up the winding polished staircase and along a hallway

"This is your room, Miss," Riccardo opened the door to a bedroom and gestured for her to enter.

"Please, call me Sarah, Miss just doesn't suit me," Sarah gasped as she studied her new room. There was a king size bed for her and a large closet. The room was decorated in beiges and creams. It was beautiful, but she loved pinks and blues and knew she needed color to brighten up her room.

"Oh, my goodness," Sarah stepped out onto her small private balcony and looked out.

"It looks like paradise."

Acres and acres of fig trees, olive trees, grape vines, and a large outdoor swimming pool.

"How do you like the room?"

Sarah squealed and whirled around,

"Oh, you scared me," she laughed, bringing a hand to her chest.

"I didn't mean to," Enrique said, his mouth turned down and his tone like ice. "Well?"

Sarah studied the man in front of her; she didn't understand why he was acting so coldly towards her. His behavior was so mercurial.

Remembering his original question, she turned her back on him to face her view and opened her arms, "I love it. How could you not, with a view like this?"

"Well, I'll…" unpack now were the next words Sarah had planned to say, but she lost them as she turned to re-enter her room, running straight into Enrique. He must have moved next to her, and she hadn't seen him.

"Oh," Sarah cried, falling backward, she put her hands out to regain her balance.

Her boss's arms wrapped around her, saving her from falling on the balcony. Heat swirled between them, then they froze.

Sarah couldn't breathe as she stared up into Enrique's eyes, then his lips came down on hers like a tidal wave. He took control of the kiss like a master, pulling her against his aroused body. She melted under him as she had known she would, her tentative hands moving to lay on his chest.

He deepened the kiss, dipping his tongue into her mouth, sliding it along her tongue until she moaned wantonly against him.

Then it ended, as abruptly as it had begun.

"Mierda," Enrique swore, pulling back.

"I'm sorry, that should not have happened," Enrique muttered, taking responsibility for their kiss as though it had been a major mistake.

Unfair.

He turned away from her and faced his vineyard. "You unpack, and I'll introduce Amalia to you at dinner time. You have two hours," Enrique told her, turning to look straight into her eyes. She could feel how hot her cheeks were and she knew she must look as though she'd been thoroughly kissed.

There was no sign on Enrique of the passion they had shared. He had pulled on his business armor. She nodded her head and folded her arms over her chest. He turned and left.

Sarah had to bite her lip to stop the tears from overflowing as he walked away, shutting the door behind him.

What had been the point of that? To kiss her so thoroughly and then to just leave as though she'd done something wrong.

Enrique Martinez was an enigma, and she didn't understand him at all.

"Sarah, may I help you unpack?"

Sarah heard Riccardo's voice and quickly pulled herself together.

Smiling was an effort, but she managed.

"No, but thank you. I have to know where I've put everything, or I'll never find it again."

Riccardo smiled at her and quietly left the room.

Sarah grinned; she had gotten a smile from him. Well, from the butler Riccardo, Enrique would be a much harder case to crack. After he had kissed her, she had seen the revulsion in his face. Was he disgusted with how wantonly she had responded to him? Or was he angry with himself for touching the 'help'? No more tempting fate.

She would stay out of sight and make sure her clothes were as conservative as possible. Sarah laughed aloud at her thoughts. The most seductive thing she owned was her cotton singlet, so that was hardly going to be a problem.

SARAH TOOK a deep calming breath and entered the dining room at the designated time. She hadn't known how formal Enrique would be dressed, so she had worn a knee length black skirt, flat ballet slippers, and a gray turtleneck cotton jumper.

She took one look at him in his beautifully tailored black pants and crisp pale blue shirt and knew she was underdressed. She smiled to herself.

She was the nanny, not his date. No need to compare her state of dress to her boss.

"Mr. Martinez," Sarah nodded her head and smiled.

"Miss Louis."

Sarah was conscious of the way his eyes ran over her figure. His mouth had tightened at the edges as though he were upset with her. But why would that be?

"I'm sorry if I'm not wearing the right thing, Mr. Martinez. May I go back and change?"

She watched his eyes widen in horror before he rushed to stop her.

"No, please don't, Miss Louis. What you are wearing is perfectly suitable."

"Well, that certainly puts me in my place," Sarah said without thinking, biting her cheeky tongue in punishment.

"Well…Your place in my household is my niece's nanny, Miss Louis. You needn't dress up. Your role does not require it."

Sarah inclined her head, focusing on the pain in her mouth. She knew he thought her inferior to him and her unveiled comment had asked for that reprimand.

"I'm sorry, you're right," Sarah looked down at the floor.

She heard Enrique draw in a huge breath.

"Amalia is being brought here in about ten minutes. She usually eats at 5 pm in her dining room before she goes to bed at 6 pm. I…" he motioned to the beautiful grandfather wall clock that stood to the side of them, "eat at 8 pm. You may choose when you would like to eat, although I believe it would best if you ate with Amalia most nights."

Enrique had a slight edge to his voice that Sarah recognized. The boss was back, and she would be doing as she was told. Of course, she'd eat with Amalia. Every night.

"She has been kept up to meet you, although I understand she is a little grumpy."

Sarah nodded her head in understanding.

She could hardly believe this was the same person who had kissed her so intensely her head was still spinning two hours later. He looked like he was carved out of stone.

Enrique's face changed, softening ever so slightly as he looked over Sarah's shoulder.

"Sarah, this is Amalia," Enrique introduced the young girl who was being brought to the room by a young maid. Sarah's heart broke. Amalia looked asleep on her little slipper covered feet.

"Amalia," Enrique addressed his niece from his position without moving, "This is Sarah. She is going to be looking after you from now on."

"I…wan…mummy," Amalia sniffed, tears welling up in her beautiful green eyes. Enrique's niece had a cherub face and eyelashes so long they fanned her plump cheeks.

Sarah moved over to her new charge and squatted down in front of Amalia, knowing, unlike Enrique, that first impressions were crucial with a child of this age. It would take her forever to gain her trust if she lost it now.

"Amalia, I'm not here to take care of you." Sarah softly corrected

Enrique. She didn't dare look behind her for fear of turning to stone. "I'm here to play with you and tell you stories, and draw with you and go swimming with you," Sarah exclaimed to the child in a soft but excited tone.

Amalia looked up from the spot on the floor where her eyes fixed.

"Really?" she asked incredulously. "Do you want to play now?"

Sarah laughed and was rewarded when the little girl smiled gently.

"It's too dark outside to play now, but I could come tuck you into bed and tell you a bedtime story if you'd like. Your uncle doesn't mind if I skip dinner, does he?" Sarah turned from her squatting position to look up at Enrique.

"Of course." Enrique nodded solemnly.

"Shall we?" Sarah held out her arms and picked up the beautiful child. Amalia went into her arms without hesitation. Sarah sighed happily as Amalia nuzzled into her neck, so she carried her towards the door without a backward glance. This was why she was here, and her heart swelled with happiness.

ENRIQUE WAS LEFT in the dining room alone. As you always are, he reminded himself. And how you want it to be.

He sat down at the head of the table, awaiting the feast he knew the cook had prepared for his return home. He ate his soup, uninterested in his favorite meal, unable to get the beautiful picture out of his head that Sarah had made carrying his niece in her arms.

Chapter Four

AMALIA WAS THE MOST INTELLIGENT, GORGEOUS LITTLE GIRL SARAH HAD ever met. Because Amalia had been born in Australia, she spoke mostly English. The day Sarah found out Amalia could not communicate properly with the staff; she made some phone calls and organized a tutor. They both began Spanish lessons the next day.

Sarah was determined that neither she nor Amalia would be disadvantaged by not speaking the language of the country in which they both now lived. Amalia should learn of her lineage and the culture of her parents and her grandparents.

Despite Amalia's clever mind, she also had quite a temper, much as Sarah expected ran in the family. But Sarah was learning how to handle her frequent outbursts. Amalia loved to swim and swimming in the family outdoor pool became the reward for her good behavior. If Amalia was good throughout the day, then she got to swim before dinner. The days she threw a tantrum, she didn't swim. It worked very well.

Sarah loved everything about her new job. The staff were wonderful and the grounds spacious, well-groomed, and open to her for exploring. She rarely saw Enrique, which relieved her. After the way he had kissed her the first day on her balcony, Sarah had to assume that he was choosing to stay as far away from her as possible.

When she did have to see him, Sarah treated Enrique with the distant respect her employer deserved. She made it her duty to find Enrique every night so that Amalia could say goodnight to him. Neither her charge nor her boss liked or appreciated the ritual. However, Sarah was not to be discouraged.

Amalia was shy of her 'big uncle', and Enrique seemed equally fearful of having any contact with his niece. That had to change. Even if it meant she had to find Enrique and physically see him every day. It was worth risking her sanity to see if a relationship could develop between them.

It was a late afternoon in her third week as Amalia's nanny. She was strolling with Amalia over to the pool for her evening swim after another beautiful day when she froze, her stomach lurching inside her body.

They were not the only ones wanting to use the pool.

Standing at one end of the Mediterranean blue tiled pool, clad only in a pair of swimming shorts, was Enrique.

He had the most perfect body Sarah had ever seen in real life. Large, broad shoulders, a well-defined chest with a flat stomach, and large biceps. His Spanish skin was a bronzed gold that shone in the afternoon sun, making him look more like a monument to a god than a man.

The heat from the sun moved inside, melting her center, and transferring to the place between her legs.

Oh damn! How am I going to get out of this?

"You've been such a good girl today, Amalia," Sarah crooned to her charge. There would be no going back on her promise, but maybe she could get Enrique to come back in half an hour?

Holding tightly to Amalia's hand, Sarah gripped her courage tight and walked up to the pool's edge.

"Mr. Martinez," Sarah greeted the pin-up that stood in front of her. "Beautiful day," she added, squinting under the strong European sun, still bright late in the day.

Enrique seemed to be holding his breath; his chest wasn't even moving. His brow furrowed as he stared at Amalia.

"Amalia, greet your uncle, please," Sarah encouraged softly, squeezing her hand gently.

"Hello, Uncle Enrique," came Amalia's small voice from beside her.

Enrique looked down to his niece and smiled.

"Good afternoon to you both. Wanting to go for a swim, are you?"

"Sarah's gon' to 'wim wit' me," came the small excited reply.

Sarah smiled apologetically at Enrique.

"Amalia, maybe we can come back after your uncle has finished his swim?" Sarah suggested.

"Noooooooooooooo," came the emotive response. "I… good, you swim, too!"

Looking over at Enrique, Amalia announced,

"We can all swim together."

"Of course, we can all swim together, chiquita," Enrique crooned.

"Chi..qui..ta?" Amalia asked.

"It means tiny girl," Enrique beamed at his niece.

Amalia beamed back at him, and Sarah gave Enrique one of her best smiles. She loved it when he tried hard with his niece. It was so easy to make her happy; he just had to put in a little bit of effort.

"Enjoy your swim girls."

Sarah watched in envy as Enrique dove head first into the cold water of the large pool and started a smooth freestyle stroke as soon as he emerged from the water. She wished she had a technique that looked like that.

"Amalia, I know I promised we could swim, but I'm not sure I can. How 'bout we swim twice as long tomorrow?"

"You promised," Amalia's lip quivered, and her eyes dropped to the ground.

Sarah sighed loudly. She was stuck.

"Well, if I promised, then I have to do it, don't I?" Sarah pulled the sunscreen out of her bag and applied a generous amount to the now wiggling child.

"A promise is a promise," Amalia sung.

Sarah sighed again, one of her lessons. Pity Amalia couldn't forget it for one day.

"Put your floaties on, good girl. Now, wait for me so I can help you into the shallow end."

Sarah took a fast breath and stripped off her modest t–shirt and cotton shorts. She only had one bathing suit. A red halter neck bikini top and matching bottoms.

"I can't believe I'm doing this," Sarah muttered to herself before running over to slide into the pool.

"In you get," Sarah called to Amalia, holding her arms up for the child to get into the water. Amalia immediately jumped into the cold pool and into her arms. She loved that the little girl trusted her so much.

"Okay, kick your legs, good girl," Sarah held Amalia as she swam across the water on her belly.

"Excellent Amalia, you are doing so well," Sarah encouraged her charge as she kicked and mimicked swimming movements.

"You've managed ten whole minutes swimming by yourself; I think that's a record."

"Me good!" Amalia shouted, hurling herself into Sarah's arms.

"Yes, you are baby," She stroked the cold child.

"Amalia," Dora called loudly from the back of the house. Dora was a maid who adored Amalia.

"Theodora," Amalia cried, grappling for the edge of the pool.

Sarah lifted her out of the water, jumping carefully up after her. Drying the little girl quickly Sarah said, "Be careful not to slip, and I'll see you at dinner." Sarah released her and watched the chubby child she had grown to adore race to the door where Dora waited.

"Don't you go with her?" came a deep voice from behind her.

Turning slowly to face the voice, Sarah self-consciously slipped back into the water. Why hadn't she gone into the town and bought herself a black one-piece?

"No, Theodora always bathes Amalia and gets her ready for dinner while I do a few laps of the pool. I'm there for her dinner, though."

"You swim every day?" Enrique enquired, cocking his head on an angle.

"Almost. Swimming before dinner is Amalia's reward for not having a tantrum– which she tended to do when I first got here. I love to swim and think it is great for her."

She was talking too much and too fast, but that tended to happen when she was around Enrique. One of the main reasons she didn't spend time with him. She turned into a loose-tongued idiot.

"Oh," was the only response she received.

Sarah walked towards the deeper end, moving her arms to keep from getting cold.

"I hope it's okay that we use the pool, Mr. Martinez. I asked Riccardo; I didn't think to ask you."

Enrique shook his head. "Amalia is my niece, and you look after her. Of course, you may use any part of the grounds you like."

Enrique looked relaxed in the pool. No frown lines, no visible stress to his body, he looked… happy.

"You like to swim, too?"

Enrique smiled, his brilliant white teeth flashing in the sunlight. "I love to swim, but rarely get time."

"And today…" Sarah led him to continue.

"And today…" Enrique mimicked her tone, smiling at her again. "I wasn't getting any work done in my office so decided to clear my head."

"And you feel better now?" Sarah breathed the question mere feet from Enrique. Her heart had begun to pound, and her nipples had tightened in the cold water.

THE ATTRACTION between them was too strong. As Sarah's pupils dilated with arousal despite the intense sun, Enrique's manhood throbbed with longing. It hardened as he gazed at her open mouth, short, sharp breaths coming in and out of her lips.

Was she waiting for him to make a move? Since her lush pink mouth was open in invitation, it seemed likely.

Enrique blindly reached out his arms, his fingers connecting with warm flesh and pulled her closer. Sarah slid her small hands up his chest, and Enrique sighed at the welcome feel of her touch. He pulled her close and her legs opened, wrapping them around his waist in the deep water.

She stared into his eyes, her lower lip trembling. He couldn't wait a moment longer. His mouth descended on hers, a sweet moan reaching his ears as he grabbed her ample bottom and pulled her tightly against him.

"God, I need this," Enrique pulled back to groan against her mouth.

Three weeks of knowing Sarah slept down the hall from him had almost driven him mad. He wanted to know her taste again. He hadn't gotten near enough the first time they had kissed. It had only made him hungry for more.

She gripped his neck tighter as his tongue plunged the inner cavities of her mouth, tasting sweetness and spice. Perfection, all in one kiss.

Sarah moaned and pushed down against him. Enrique groaned. He could feel her entrance. If they were naked, they would be making love already.

Heat rolled over his neck and down his spine, exploding sensation along his nerves. He'd never wanted anyone so badly. He kissed her deeply again as he moved his hand beneath her bathers, slipping his fingers in to caress the slick folds. She was wet and ready for him. A groan vibrated in his throat.

She's so ready. Enrique pushed two fingers into her, hot, tight body squeezing him tight. Sarah arched upwards, breaking their kiss, and moaning loudly. Wantonly.

As Sarah broke the kiss, Enrique's surroundings came pounding into his consciousness like a hammer to his eyeballs.

He was in his pool.

In his backyard.

With the nanny in his arms.

Not only that, his fingers were still inside her! *It's daylight for Christ's sakes. You could have been seen by anyone.*

Removing his fingers gently, Enrique pulled Sarah softly back down from her arched position. She opened her eyes, and Enrique looked down into beautiful blue, passion-dazed eyes and lost his heart.

His breath was still coming hard, and although he had used all of his strength to bring back his impassive face, his body was shaking from the strain of it.

Why couldn't he just carry her out of the water and do what they both needed so much?

Because she's a servant, you fool. Don't be an idiot.

Sarah's lip trembled, and Enrique's heart sank. If she cried, he would have to apologize.

He never apologized.

"Sarah, she'll be down in ten minutes," Theodora called from the house.

"I better go."

Enrique ached to pull her back into his arms as she scrambled out of them. But instead, he just nodded and turned away as Sarah jumped out of the pool, collected her clothes and ran for the house without a backward glance.

Chapter Five

"It has been far too long since I had a party, Sofia," Enrique told his local assistant over his cell phone. "I want you to organize a cocktail party for ten friends next Saturday night."

"At your home, sir?"

"Yes, of course. The works, music, drinks, tell the chef to go all out."

Sophia was quiet as she wrote everything down.

"Would you like me to send out any of the invitations, sir?" She asked.

Enrique thought about that.

"No, I will. Ten people."

"Male, Female, a combination? For catering purposes."

Enrique smiled devilishly. "Five of each. That's everything."

Enrique grinned as he hung up the phone.

The image of Sarah in that tiny red bikini still tormented his dreams at night when he was alone in his cold bed. He couldn't seem to forget the way she had felt beneath his hands, the way she had tasted on his lips. If it was just a physical need to have sex with her, he could have handled that. But this constant need to see her, watch her smile. It was infuriating him. He was acting like some lovesick school boy.

Getting his closest friends together would be the perfect way to make him remember what was important to him and who was important in his life.

ENRIQUE HADN'T SEEN Sarah all day, and he was grateful for the respite. Conference calls with the office in London had kept him busy all day. He was stressed enough without having to worry about little Miss Sunshine appearing to disarm his brain.

He smiled wearily to himself, realizing how close to the truth his joking assessment of her was. She was little Miss Sunshine to him. Bringing light into his otherwise dull world.

Not tonight, though.

Tonight, he would forget her.

Enrique strode off for the shower and to change for his party.

Enrique's guests arrived at the house promptly at 5:30 pm. Sofia had organized a string quartet to play music throughout the night, and he smiled at the way the house had been decked out for this evening.

His chef had prepared amazing appetizers and a three-course meal. There was a huge assortment of drinks, and a bar had been set up where a staff member would be serving drinks all night to his guests.

Perhaps it was a little overkill for only ten people, but Enrique wanted to spoil himself. If he couldn't go to London, he would bring the atmosphere and luxury to him.

"Enrique, *como estas?*"

Valentina.

Enrique tried not to flinch when her pseudo-sultry tones floated into the air. The most beautiful woman at the party. With platinum blonde, shoulder length hair and amazing green eyes, she was the envy of every woman who knew her. She sashayed up to him, tiny hips swaying suggestively in her skin tight black dress.

"*Estoy bien*, Valentina. *Como estas?*" Enrique replied.

"*Estoy satisfecho, gracias*," Valentina purred again, air kissing either side of his face, barely millimeters away from Enrique's mouth.

Enrique tried not to grin too broadly. He knew Valentina wanted him. She had made it obvious over the years, but tempting as it had been on occasion, Enrique had never indulged. He knew her parents well, and there was no future for them. She wasn't what he wanted in a wife.

So why would he hurt her, and inadvertently insult her parents in the interim?

Enrique chatted with his friend Mateo, laughing at his friend's story about his latest conquest.

Mateo was a known ladies' man amongst their inner circle. He had perfect taste in women, clothes, and the stock market– some of the main reasons Enrique liked him.

"Who is that?" Mateo asked, his eyes twinkling with mischief.

Enrique froze and counted to three before turning around slowly.

He knew who was behind him.

"Sarah," Enrique breathed, watching the object of his dreams walk through the dining room door and head straight towards him, Amalia in her arms.

She wore a plain pink t–shirt and denim shorts, looking out of place in his party.

She smiled at Enrique, looking directly up into his eyes.

"I'm sorry to interrupt you, Mr. Martinez, but Amalia has come to say good night to you."

She hoisted Amalia up on her hip and gave her an encouraging smile.

"You can do it," Sarah whispered into her ear.

Enrique's friends were all staring at her now, and Sarah blushed red at their obvious attention.

"*Buenas Noches, mi tio*," Amalia whispered, her eyes downcast.

Enrique was taken aback but quickly recovered himself. He smiled gratefully at Sarah.

"*Bien hecho*, Amalia," Enrique praised his niece, a few ooh's and aah's coming from his female guests. Amalia lifted her head and looked at him, then noticing everyone staring at her, cuddled closer into Sarah's chest. Amalia whispered a question into Sarah's ear, and Enrique saw Sarah's eyes grow worried.

She smiled gently and said to Amalia, "You can tell your uncle whatever you like."

"*Te amo*," Amalia whispered.

Enrique's gut wrenched at the innocent words. He had not expected to hear them and he froze. However hard he tried; no words would come out of his mouth.

Sarah's eyes were on him, pleading with him to return the words.

"Your uncle loves you too, sweetie. And you said that so perfectly, I am so proud of you."

Sarah tucked Amalia's head into the crook of her neck protectively and gave Enrique a stare that would have withered a twenty-foot cactus. Then she walked away.

"Who was that amazing creature?" Mateo asked Enrique in Spanish, his eyes running up and down the length of Sarah's body as she walked away.

"Amalia's nanny," Enrique told his friend, still reeling from the shock of what had just happened.

"Why didn't you invite her to the party? She'd probably be more fun than these stuffy bitches," Mateo sneered. "Did you see the death stare, though? Are you sure she works for you?"

As Mateo walked off chuckling, Enrique knew his friend had observed the exchange between them correctly. Sarah never hid her feelings. You could read her face like a book. She'd been like that when he'd kissed her. She hadn't held her feelings back, showing him just how much she wanted him, too. The honesty that was such an integral part of her character floored Enrique every time; she was so unique.

She treated him like an equal, a man, no more, no less. And in his world of wealth and power, she was as refreshing as the cool breeze blowing across a desert at night.

SARAH CARRIED AMALIA TO BED, her arms shaking with the strength not to scream in frustration. She was so proud of the little girl in her arms and yet so unbelievably angry with the fully-grown man who couldn't tell his niece how he felt about her. It wouldn't have taken much to appease her. An 'I love you too' would have been enough. *Hardly brain surgery.*

Sarah snorted aloud.

She could just see the headline now. *'Legendary Spanish playboy and business wizard– a stuffed dummy when accosted by a three-year-old little girl's love!'*

He was either one of those men that just didn't say *'I love you,'* or he was so moved by Amalia's expression that he was stunned into silence. She hoped it was the latter.

Sarah headed back to the main part of the house once Amalia was settled and asleep. She had a few hours to fill before she went to bed herself. Maybe she would go to her bedroom and read. She had found the library at the Martinez manor and was currently reading about Ancient Spanish history.

Sarah snuck into the main area hoping to go unnoticed. She made it half way up the staircase when she heard an unfamiliar male voice.

"Enrique, your nanny's back. Why don't you ask her to join us?"

"I'm Mateo Rodriguez."

Sarah gripped the railing for a moment, considering ignoring him and walking up to her room. But good manners forbade her that, so she turned around and found herself smiling slowly at the handsome man standing in the foyer. His eyes told her he was kind, but there was a mischievous streak she recognized far too well. Sarah heard the warning in her head. *This could get messy.*

"I'm Sarah Louis."

"Sarah, I was hoping you would join us for a drink." Mateo invited her charmingly with perfect English. He gestured towards the dining room and bowed in polite invitation.

"I'm afraid I can't. I'm not dressed appropriately." Sarah gave him the easiest excuse she could think of and gestured to her denim shorts and short sleeved shirt.

"You can change, then come back down," Mateo suggested.

"No, I don't think so, but thank you." Sarah took two more steps up the staircase. She may have gotten away with it. Relief filled her belly with bubbles. Then she heard his voice.

"You are welcome to stay."

Enrique. Sarah swallowed hard. Turning back around to look down upon the men, her boss walking into the foyer.

"I've already eaten, and I was hoping to get a little reading done tonight," Sarah told him, crossing her arms over her chest. "I thought I'd work on more of my Spanish, for Amalia." She narrowed her eyes at him in silent reprimand.

"Well, I have an easy compromise. You could read for a little while, get changed into something more appropriate and meet us back here about nine?" Mateo suggested, giving Enrique a nudge.

"Ahh, yes. You could do that," Enrique slowly agreed. "In fact, I think you should join us, Sarah."

She considered her options. It was either offending Enrique and his friend or put up with a few hours of small talk and cocktails. Not a great choice, either way she looked at it, but what the hell?

"Sounds like a plan," Sarah announced brightly, flicking her pony-tail over her shoulder. "See you around nine."

And with that bright note and a quick glance at Enrique's steely expression she headed up to her room.

Sarah sat in her bath for an hour. What would she have to talk to Enrique's guests about? And she only had one thing to wear. Would they think she was a joke in her little green dress? All the women downstairs wore black. Maybe Mateo and Enrique wouldn't notice if she didn't show up?

The image of Enrique in her bedroom again asking after her was enough to spur her out of the bath. She would rather spend the evening talking to his friends than risk another encounter alone with him.

Sarah washed and blow dried her long hair and carefully applied what little makeup she owned. Then came the dress. Standing in only her cotton undies, she stared at the dress hanging up in her wardrobe. Did she dare wear it? She didn't have much of a choice. She'd told them she needed to change into something more appropriate and there was obviously a set dress code for the night.

Sarah put her new cocktail dress on and her only pair of small black heels took a deep breath and headed down the stairs.

ENRIQUE SENSED her before he saw her. He stiffened when the hairs on his arms prickled and reluctantly turned around to watch her approach through the doors.

He stopped breathing. It was much worse than he had anticipated. She looked more beautiful than any other woman in the room.

Her knee length dress clung to her curves, and the halter neck showed off her creamy skin and spectacular shape.

Guau. Wow.

"Oh *guau*," Mateo said aloud. Enrique couldn't have agreed with his friend more. He was in big trouble where this girl was concerned.

"Mr. Martinez, I'm sorry I'm a little late," Sarah apologized.

"I think tonight we should call each other by our first names. You are, after all, my guest this evening." Enrique murmured, his eyes drinking her in like an addictive drug. God, she was beautiful. She shone like the sun.

"Ummm," Sarah hesitated. "Okay, Enrique," Sarah smiled, testing the word on her tongue.

"Sarah, you look incredible," Mateo gushed, stepping out from behind Enrique to pick up one of Sarah's hands and kiss it. Sarah blushed, and Enrique clenched his fists behind his back.

He had to stop himself from pulling her hand from his friend's grasp.

"Thank you," Sarah spoke to Mateo, her eyes glistening after his compliment.

Mateo smiled smugly.

"Can I get you a drink?" Mateo asked.

"Yes please, I'd love a red wine if I could, please."

As Mateo trotted off for her drink, Enrique couldn't hide his surprise at her choice.

"You drink red wine?" Enrique asked, knowing the answer was obvious.

"Yes, I love it. I'm just not a big drinker."

Sarah lowered her eyes to her dress and smoothed out a wrinkle; she looked uncomfortable and self-conscious. He wasn't surprised; she'd been eyed off by every male and female in the room.

"You do look lovely," Enrique whispered to her

Her head came up with a snap, and she looked deep into Enrique's eyes. Was she searching for his sincerity?

"Well, thank you. But with a body like mine, dresses that fit like this are few and far between."

Sarah was a few sizes bigger than the women in the room, but her natural voluptuousness was one of her biggest assets. It made her different than everyone else, and that difference made her special, at least in his eyes.

"There's nothing wrong with your body, Sarah." How could she think so lowly of herself? She was so beautiful it was staggering.

Mateo came forward with a glass of wine for Sarah.

"What did I miss?" he asked.

"Oh, not much," Sarah laughed. "Enrique just tried to make me feel more comfortable. Since I obviously stand out like a sore thumb in this room," Sarah giggled again, gesturing around her.

"Hardly, Sarah," Mateo murmured, allowing his eyes a slow perusal of her dress. His facial expression was walking a fine line between awe and lust.

Lowering his voice again he whispered, "You make all these other women look like dull, uninspiring twigs."

Enrique stared at his friend. He knew for a fact that Mateo had already slept with half the women at the party. How could he find Sarah attractive?

Well, how do you find Sarah attractive when she's so different to the usual women you date?

Sarah blushed again, and Enrique growled.

Mateo looked up and winked. *He winked!*

Huh? Did Mateo have an inkling about the feelings Enrique was fighting in regard to Sarah? Was his attraction to her that obvious?

"Let me introduce you to some people," Mateo said, offering Sarah his arm.

Sarah linked her arm in Mateo's without hesitation and walked away with him.

Enrique stared after them, still in shock that his best friend would dare flirt with the one woman that he wanted. He hadn't quite worked out how the attraction with Sarah was going to work, but he certainly didn't want Mateo anywhere near her.

SARAH COULDN'T BELIEVE how much attention she was receiving from Mateo. He was handsome and very charming. However, the only man she had ever wanted in her heart and her bed was on the other side of the room.

The rest of the night passed quickly as she made small talk with some of the most beautiful people she had ever seen in real life. All of them were successful, stunning, and came from money. It was evident that Enrique didn't stray far from his pond.

Sarah should have felt like a fish out of water, but that was hard with Mateo there, by her side the whole night. Always offering a compliment or a hand around her waist when necessary.

It was lovely, but if only Enrique would come over and speak to her also. She turned to look behind her for what felt like the hundredth time that night and saw Enrique standing alone. Sarah gathered her courage and excused herself from the group she was speaking with.

She smiled as she approached and Enrique returned the look. His eyes rested on her unrestrained breasts, and she lifted her chest higher. If anything was going to happen between them, tonight was the night.

Valentina, a blonde stick insect that she didn't like, chose that exact time to drape her lovely body all over Enrique.

"*Querida,*" she purred, loud enough for Sarah to hear as she wrapped her arms around his neck and gyrated against his body.

"I have enjoyed myself tonight," she said, lifting her mouth up to his to be kissed.

Acid dropped and curdled in the pit of Sarah's stomach. She couldn't watch that. She turned away from the sight with tears prickling her eyes, only to run straight into the gym developed chest of Mateo.

She stared at his tie, unable to lift her head in case he saw the tears she knew would be visible now.

"Shall we go outside, beautiful?" he asked gently.

Sarah couldn't speak so she just nodded her head, and Mateo took her hand, steering her outside onto the balcony. The air was still warm, but Sarah shivered as she blinked her eyes and took a deep breath.

You're being ridiculous. Stop it.

"Are you okay, Sarah?" Mateo asked her.

"Oh, fine. Just one too many red wines, I think," Sarah laughed off his question, wiping the tears from her cheeks and sinking into one of the seats adorning the balcony. Her legs were close to buckling.

"I am glad you chose to join us, Sarah. You have been a breath of fresh air for me tonight."

Sarah blushed for the tenth time, heat spreading across her cheeks. Mateo's compliments were so flowery. She wasn't used to it.

"Thank you, but I don't know how you can say that truthfully. I..." Sarah stopped and took a breath. She shouldn't take her anger out on Mateo. "I'm not thin and sophisticated like those women. I don't have some fancy career to impress you. I don't know why you've bothered with me all night." A half sob rose from Sarah's throat on her last words and she swallowed it down. *How embarrassing.*

Mateo laughed, he laughed! She lifted her head and frowned at him, then he sat down next to her, put his arm around her and gave her a comforting squeeze.

The anger that had risen for a moment died a quick death, and she leaned into him.

"Sarah, you are more beautiful than all of those women because you are different. Your passion for your career is inspiring, and your heart is warm."

Sarah smiled, a solitary tear falling onto her cheek.

"Oh, I'm sorry, I don't know what's wrong with me." Wiping away the tear, Sarah tried for a laugh that came out half choked. Again, Mateo gave that soft chuckle.

"I do, and if you and Enrique don't get your act together, I will be very disappointed in you both."

Sarah twisted around and stared at Mateo, stunned into speechlessness. *He didn't believe...*

"I don't know what you mean," she gasped, trying for a sophisticated reply, and failing miserably.

"You know exactly what I mean, and I might say I am a little bit envious of my old friend. It's not every day a girl like you walks into our lives."

His tone was joking and yet his eyes seemed serious.

"Oh, I...." Sarah was caught, what could she say to that? "You are very kind Mateo; I have appreciated everything you have done for me tonight, but..."

"Yeah, I know," Mateo laughed again.

He grasped Sarah's chin and touched his lips to hers briefly before saying, "Let's get back in there."

What was it with these Spanish men? Did she have a stamp on her forehead saying, 'needs to be kissed'?

ENRIQUE WATCHED THEM RE–ENTER the room. Sarah looked different than when she had gone out onto the balcony. There was a slight warmth in her cheeks and her lip gloss was coloring Mateo's mouth.

He should have, and could have, run over there and punched his best friend in his no-good face! It took every bit of strength Enrique possessed not to run out after them once he had removed Valentina from his body and handed her off to another one of his friends.

Mateo made eye contact with him and smiled. "I think it's time to go," Mateo shouted, calling to the people in the room like a goat herder.

There was a mumble about *'look at the time'* and all of a sudden, they were all packing up to leave.

"Thanks, amigo," Mateo said to Enrique, shaking his hand, and smiling.

Enrique couldn't return the smile. "Hope you had a good time."

"I did actually. Best party you've ever had." There was that mischievous grin again. Mateo leaned forward and said, "I just had to have a little taste old friend, she is single, right?"

Enrique's grip tightened.

There was a chorus of goodbyes, and they were all gone.

"I uh, think, I'll go to bed," Sarah said from behind him, her timid words fueling the anger inside him.

Enrique's hard-won control exploded as the whiskey took full effect on him.

"You let him kiss you!" Enrique roared, whirling around to face her.

"Why shouldn't I?" Sarah challenged him, setting her chin in defiance.

"Do you know how many women he's been with? He will chew you up and spit you out like every one of his whores." Enrique bit out the words, letting his temper and his jealousy run away with his good sense.

Whack, the palm of her hand landed a clean blow across his cheek, fire exploding across his face.

Bursting into tears, Sarah ran from the room.

What on Earth had he just done?

Chapter Six

ENRIQUE STOOD IN THE DINING ROOM FOR AT LEAST FIVE MINUTES after Sarah had run from the room, playing the night over in his head. How could he have been so cruel to her? She had come to the party at his request. She had dressed up for his party– when she never dressed up. She had talked to and impressed his friends– not at all an easy task.

He knew why he had been so mean to her; he was jealous. A shudder rippled through him in recognition of the truth.

Jealous of the way Mateo had touched her throughout the night. Jealous of the attention Mateo was allowed to give her while he, Enrique, had to stand back and watch.

Thinking back on what he'd witnessed after their supposed kiss, Sarah's lips had not been swollen, there had not been a fuzzy look in her eyes, and her hair had still looked perfect. Apparently, Mateo hadn't kissed her for long or with much passion.

He clenched his fist and tore it through the air in exasperation.

Why was it that every time Sarah was around, he forgot she was Amalia's nanny? He paid her to be here, why couldn't he feel the same way about her as he did everybody else in his employ?

Amalia loves this woman.

A horrible realization hit him with the weight of a fist in his stomach. What if Sarah wanted to quit because of what he had said to her? He couldn't have that. It would destroy his niece. It was this justification that spurred Enrique up to her bedroom.

He lifted his hand and knocked on her door twice before daring to speak.

"Sarah, please open the door. I need to talk to you."

Sarah opened the door, looking positively horrible. Her nose was bright red, her cheeks blotchy.

"Can I come in?" Enrique asked, not wanting his whole house to hear him apologize to her in the hallway.

"It's your house," Sarah tossed back at him, throwing her hands up in the air.

"I shouldn't have said what I said to you just now," Enrique admitted, stepping into her room and shutting the door behind him. She'd made changes to his guest bedroom. The traditional watercolor paintings had been taken down and in their place were enlarged photos of what Enrique had to assume were her parents and her friends.

There was also a handmade quilt on the bed that Enrique had never seen before. The room didn't look like it belonged in his house anymore, it looked like her.

And it felt more like home than any other room in his house.

He coughed, clearing his throat as he squashed his tender thoughts into a tiny box in his mind where they belonged.

"Then why did you, Enrique? Please tell me. Because no one has ever said such a horrible thing to me before. Never."

"Well, I…" Enrique stopped.

"Well?" Sarah demanded, hands on her hips, legs spread wide. She was a real sight standing in the middle of her room.

"Well?" she practically screamed.

"I was jealous! Okay?" Enrique roared back at her. He turned his back on her, his pulse thundering in his ears.

"But why?" Sarah asked, her tone surprised.

"Why?" Enrique repeated, spinning back around to face her. How could she not understand?

In two strides, he covered the room and took her into his arms. He wrapped his hands around her waist and pulled her against him. Sarah didn't fight him. Instead, she thrust her fingers into his hair and fed on his mouth as he fed on hers. She met his force with an equal strength as their tongues mated and his hands roamed over her body.

Sarah gasped into his mouth as his hand found her breast. The nipple tightened under his palm, and she moaned as his thumb teased the point into puckering even more. Enrique broke the kiss and looked down on her.

"I want you so much. Tell me if you don't want this, please." Enrique rasped, every muscle in his body coiled and ready to spring.

"You are so beautiful," Sarah whispered, staring up into his eyes.

She cupped his jaw and smiled up at him with a look on her face that he'd never seen before. Enrique's heart cracked a little.

"Beautiful? You're the one that's beautiful, Sarah, too beautiful. I couldn't keep my eyes off you tonight," he told her between kisses.

"Really?" Sarah's eyes went wide with surprise.

Enrique laughed at her shocked face, bringing a smile to Sarah's lips.

"And I have wanted to get you out of this incredible dress all night."

Sarah stilled in his arms for a moment as though she was shocked; then she stepped back from his grasp.

"Well then."

Undoing the zip behind her and unfastening the tie at her neck she let the dress slide down over her hips.

Enrique stared. She was every bit the goddess he had imagined she would be. Long, firm legs, round hips, a tiny waist, and heavy, rounded creamy breasts that were topped with strawberry nipples.

Enrique growled low in his throat. He was already hard from their passionate kissing, but it was moving towards painful.

He maneuvered Sarah towards the bed. Sitting her down, he knelt between her knees, spreading her legs wide.

She gasped and tried to pull her legs together, the move at odds with her previous strip tease.

Enrique chuckled at her nervousness; he was feeling the same way, which was totally unusual for him. He had never wanted anyone so much. The fact that he finally had her where he wanted her made him want to roar like the king of the jungle.

Enrique bent his head again and took one puckered nipple into his mouth and feasted on it. She tasted like sunshine and sweet strawberries. Sarah's back arched and her head fell back.

Enrique took his time on one breast before turning his attention to its twin, smiling at the pressure Sarah was applying to his head to keep him on her. It was evident that she wanted him as much as he wanted her.

Sarah's hands moved to the buttons of his shirt. He needed to be out of his clothes soon before they all caught on fire.

He wanted to possess Sarah, body, and soul. To fill her so completely that she would never forget him, no matter where she traveled, no matter who she was with.

His possessiveness shocked him, but he brushed off what the thought suggested and focused on her.

Standing up, Enrique stripped off his shirt, pants, and shoes, leaving only his cotton boxers in place.

She licked her lips nervously, and Enrique saw her distress, her eyes fixated on his groin where his phallus strained against the fabric.

He laughed, "Don't worry, this will work."

He pushed Sarah back until she lay on the pillows, moving his hand from her breast to the place between her legs. She stiffened against him, and he soothed her with his mouth, kissing her until she relaxed.

Enrique sat up, pulling the underwear from her body and stared down at the small strip of hair that matched the top of her head. He smiled as he realized that his original thoughts of her had been correct– impeccably groomed.

Sarah reached for his boxers and pushed them down his hips too, his rod springing free. He sighed with the relief and freedom.

Sarah pulled Enrique over her for another kiss, and he ran his hand up her inner thigh.

Sarah squealed.

"Are you okay?" Enrique asked.

"Yes, please keep going. I feel like my body's on fire."

Enrique laughed again; he loved the fact that she was so turned on by him. She couldn't hide it and didn't seem to want to.

"I know, but I want you aching even more for me."

His words held a promise in them that he intended to keep and Sarah planted frantic kisses all over his neck, running her hands down his back and around to the front of his hips.

It was Enrique's turn to pull away from her; her intensity made his chest hurt. How would he ever go back to forced oohs and ahhs after this? How would anyone else please him when he had experienced this woman?

"No fair," Sarah pouted.

"I already want you too much, I'll let you touch me later," Enrique pulled her forwards, tasting her sweet mouth once again as his fingers found the sweet spot of her desire. She moaned into his mouth and pressed herself further into Enrique's hands.

Sarah groaned again, and Enrique couldn't help himself, turning his hand over and slipping his middle finger through her slippery folds into her tight body.

Sarah's head fell back on a groan.

Enrique almost came right there next to her; she was so wet for him, and his body screamed to be inside her so badly he could barely think.

He wanted her to come first before he thrust into her. He already had the feeling he wouldn't last long. With Sarah, everything felt new and different.

There was a need to touch her, a desperation he hadn't experienced before. Her responses told him that she had never known an experienced man's touch before, nor pure pleasure. Her body was begging for the attention he knew he could give it.

He withdrew his finger and pressed his wet fingertips across the tight button again. Over and over until she was crying out to him.

Enrique lifted his head from her breast to watch her face contort. He felt her stiffen and groan and bent to kiss her neck softly.

Sarah shuddered in his arms and Enrique savored the moment. She was completely and utterly divine.

"Please..." Sarah groaned, lifting her hips in silent invitation.

Yes.

Enrique pushed himself up on top of her, parting her legs, he thrust into her in one fast movement. He heard her cry out in pain. His body registered the virginal tightness even as it welcomed him. Shocked, he went to withdraw.

Why didn't she tell me?

Sarah wrapped her legs around his waist and held him close with her strong legs.

"Please, don't stop," Sarah begged, blinking away tears.

"You should have told me," Enrique bit out, upset with himself for not knowing. And yet, she was so beautiful and twenty-six years old, how could he have known?

"Please..." Sarah begged again, squeezing her inner muscles around his throbbing length.

Enrique groaned and without thought thrust into her body again. He couldn't stop himself. Being inside her felt like coming home. Even with the shock of taking her innocence, he couldn't ignore the need in his loins. The throbbing between his legs was overriding his need to question her further. He thrust into her again slowly, allowing her body to adjust to him as he set their rhythm.

"You're okay?" Enrique whispered, watching pleasure flicker across her face.

"Enrique, you feel so good," Sarah moaned, opening her eyes to him. Her eyes were so clear that Enrique saw her heart in them. He looked away, too afraid to see what she had to give him, too scared that if he looked into her eyes, he would be caught there forever.

The tightness of her body and the sounds of pleasure she made pushed Enrique higher and higher. He picked up the speed of his thrusts, hearing her gasp and shudder around him. He could no longer hold back his orgasm, and as he released himself into her, he found a place so exquisite he lost a piece of himself to her.

As he slowly came back to himself and the tiny explosions of heat stopped flickering over his skin, he relaxed against her warm, soft body. Sarah was running her nails up and down Enrique's back in a gentle and familiar way. He didn't want to move, but he knew he had to.

He pushed himself back from her and sat back on his haunches looking down and seeing a small amount of red. Guilt washed over him.

"Please don't leave yet," Sarah begged him, sitting up and reaching out for him.

No, he would not leave her yet. If he only had tonight to be with her, then he would enjoy it to its full extent.

"I'm not going to leave you, *querida*. But I think we should have a shower; you're bleeding a little."

"Oh my god, is that normal?" She blurted out, jumping off the bed and grabbing tissues to place between her legs.

Enrique laughed gently, "I don't know, it's been a long time since I made love to a virgin."

Enrique knew he should be mad at her for not telling him, but the pride he felt knowing that she had been a virgin overpowered the anger. Sarah blushed.

"I'm sorry I didn't tell you. I didn't plan this, and then I didn't think it mattered." Sarah dropped her eyes and looked down at the ground.

"Oh, it matters, Sarah. I would have been so much gentler if I'd known." Enrique lifted her chin with his finger so that she would look at him.

"I am truly honored," he told her solemnly, the Spanish male in him puffing up his chest with pride.

"Shall we shower?" Enrique asked her, tapping her bottom in the direction of her en suite. Sarah laughed and started walking towards the bathroom.

"Ahh, do you think we should have, you know..." Sarah motioned towards his member. Enrique didn't understand what she meant, and he raised his eyebrows.

"Protection?"

A Spanish expletive hissed out between Enrique's lips.

"I cannot believe I didn't use anything."

A condom! He hadn't worn a condom. Of all the stupid things to do. In twenty years, he had never had unprotected sex with a woman. No wonder he had come so quickly. She had felt so good without that layer of artificial 'skin' between them.

"Well, I'm healthy Sarah, I get regular checks, there's nothing for you to worry about."

"Good to know," Sarah said sarcastically.

"I only meant, oh, doesn't matter," Enrique muttered, this talk was killing the atmosphere between them.

"I'm going to my room to get some protection for us; you jump in the shower. I'll meet you there." Enrique paused to see Sarah's confused face.

"You want to do it again?" she blurted out, then colored red.

Enrique grinned at her and took her into his arms once more. He kissed her soundly until they were both aroused and in need again.

"I guess so."

He tapped her on the bottom again and gathered up his underwear.

After a quick stop to his room and back again, Enrique returned to Sarah's room.

He stood in the doorway of her en suite and watched Sarah in the shower. She had her eyes closed and head back, letting the hot water run down between her breasts and over her stomach. He grew hard again just watching her. He looked down at himself in astonishment. He'd never been so quickly aroused; she was incredible for his libido.

Sarah saw him and smiled her invitation.

Enrique stepped into the double shower and drew her body up against his.

"You're not too sore?" He asked. He was still feeling guilty about having inadvertently hurt her with his lack of restraint and was anxious not to do it again.

"I'm aware of myself, but not too sore." She conceded.

Sarah picked up the soap and began washing Enrique's chest, shyly peering up at him from between her eyelashes.

"Thank you for making tonight so wonderful," Sarah told him.

His heart swelled, and he fought off the feelings surrounding what they had just done. They'd had sex. Nothing more.

His voice dropped into a serious tone.

"Sarah, I have to tell you. I cannot promise you anything except what we have right now. Is this enough for you?"

He had to be honest. Tonight would not be enough for him, but neither could he offer more than sex to her.

She smiled seductively up at him.

"We're both clean enough. We should go enjoy each other a little more."

Enrique laughed at her as she handed him a towel.

Throughout the night, Sarah kissed every inch of Enrique's body and he hers. He learned it in so much detail he could have painted it come morning.

Chapter Seven

Sarah awoke early, as she always did, and reached out for Enrique's body. He was gone. She knew he'd slept some of the night with her. She had fallen asleep in his arms.

Her body ached in places that had never ached before, and her hand floated down to her lower belly, hoping that their first love making hadn't made anything else that would not be welcomed by him.

Shaking off the unwelcome thoughts, she showered, dressed, and made her way down to Amalia.

The rest of the day flowed on like most others, except that she received a note at 6 pm accompanying the empty plate that should have contained her dinner.

'Have dinner with me tonight. See you at 8 pm.'

A note from Enrique instead of chicken and vegetables. How good was that? And in real Enrique style, it wasn't a question, it was a demand, and it made her smile.

Sarah dressed in her new white silk blouse and black skirt. If Enrique was going to make a habit of inviting her to dinner, she would have to do some more shopping.

She found her way to the dining room and Enrique was already there, standing by the fireplace waiting for her.

"Good evening," Sarah greeted him warmly. She stopped just in front of him, not quite sure how to greet him in 'public'. As usual, he looked unbelievable. Tailored gray pants and a black shirt that clung to his muscular body.

"Good evening, Sarah," Enrique tilted his head slightly towards her in greeting.

Oh… okay. So, no kissing in the dining room.

"Please, have a seat," Enrique held out the chair that sat opposite him. The long dining room table had been set for two.

Sarah smiled and sat down. Was this what it was like to be courted by a prince?

"You look lovely, once again," Enrique told her, lifting the wine glass to his lips and taking a large, seemingly nervous gulp.

"Thank you. I went shopping yesterday in the village for these. There is a beautiful boutique there that I like."

The woman had been lovely to her, and the clothes had fit so well. The Spanish designers obviously knew how to dress a woman with curves.

He grinned at her.

"Well, as I am hoping you will join me more frequently for dinner, perhaps more shopping is in order? I will set up an account for you tomorrow."

Hmmm…

"I would love to have dinner with you more often, Enrique," she said his name slowly, sounding it out for the first time today. "However, an account isn't necessary. I'll buy a few more pieces myself, then interchange them."

"I want to get you some clothes as a present, Sarah. We will go together then if you do not want an account." His dark eyebrows were drawn together as though he were displeased.

What was with that?

She didn't want to be paid in any way for sex. Why would he buy her clothes just because their relationship had changed? She knew that olden day mistresses had all their clothes bought for them by their 'protectors', and she certainly didn't want that sort of relationship.

However, not wanting to get into another argument she only said, "We'll see."

The soup was served, and she began eating, her taste buds dancing with happiness as the flavors mixed in her mouth.

The food the chef prepared was always beautiful but plain, as she ate what Amalia did most of the time.

She was enjoying the adult experience far too much.

"Do you like the soup?" Enrique asked, obviously noticing the way she was gobbling it up.

"Oh, I love it. This shrimp soup has to be my favorite."

Enrique smiled, seemingly happy with how their first 'date' was going.

"Sarah, I was hoping you would come to an agreement with me. After last night I am convinced that we both enjoy each other's company. Am I correct?"

Sarah nodded, her hands beginning to shake, so she put the spoon down. Where was he going with this?

"I cannot commit to a relationship at this point, but I was hoping we could still spend time together. I have my work during the day, and you have Amalia. But we could have dinner together and be together afterward. Would that work for you?"

Sarah stilled and forced the shock from her mind. He had just proposed an 'employer with benefits' arrangement, and she was hard pressed not to be insulted by his offer. At least he was honest with her, which was a good sign that he respected her. But could she risk falling more in love with him when she knew he would stop their liaison once he had his fill of her?

Her head screamed, *No! Don't be an idiot.* But her heart screamed *Yes– take whatever you can get!*

After waiting so many years to feel the passion that she'd experienced last night, she wasn't waiting another twenty-six years to feel it again.

"I would love that," Sarah told him, giving him one of her biggest smiles.

"Good," Enrique nodded once.

They chatted over dinner about Amalia, the food, and then headed straight to Sarah's room.

As soon as they crossed the threshold, Enrique scooped her up into his arms and carried her towards the bed.

"I'm too heavy," Sarah squealed, holding on tightly to his neck. He was going to hurt his back lifting her like he was.

Enrique just laughed.

"I want you so badly, I can hardly think." He gasped out, placing her in the middle of the queen-sized bed.

She stretched out onto her back, heat coiling into the center of her body. She loved that he wanted her. Being desired by such a good-looking man was heady indeed.

He stripped out of his clothes, his magnificent olive skin making her mouth water. She needed to taste him.

Sarah struggled out of her clothes as quickly as she could, wanting to be as close as possible to him.

As soon as she was naked, she reached out and pulled him onto the bed. It was her turn to enjoy him.

She pushed him onto his back and sat up on him, straddling his thighs and reveling in the heat of his body beneath hers. Her long hair cascaded over her shoulders, covering her breasts from his view, making her feel feminine and soft.

"My turn," Sarah announced, pinning his strong arms down in mock domination.

She'd never done anything like this before, and yet she was aching to know how every inch of his body tasted.

She began her seduction by kissing him softly on the mouth, dipping her tongue in ever so gently.

Enrique groaned but didn't stop her from continuing. Although from the expletive he uttered, she was pretty sure he wanted to.

Sarah moved down his body, kissing each flat brown nipple separately, tasting each with her tongue. She moved down his flat belly further, kissing each inch of his hard, muscular body as she slid slowly down.

Sarah finally reached his erection and stared at it, then looked up at him. Her eyes must have looked a little fearful because a choked laugh came from Enrique.

"What's wrong, *querida?*"

"Do you want me to?" Sarah wrapped her fingers around him and began stroking gently, the skin surprisingly soft.

Enrique moaned, his eyes closing.

"Well?" she asked again, determined he would answer her question.

Enrique groaned again, louder this time and thrust his hips up in apparent frustration.

He glanced at her and told her quickly, "Yes," before laying back again to avoid looking at her.

"How much?" Sarah asked as she stroked him further.

He gasped as he grew even bigger and impossibly hard under her unpracticed fingers.

"Sarah, please," he begged, hips arching up again in invitation.

A swell of pride crashed against her at his pleading tone, and she dipped her head, smiling to herself.

She had wanted to taste him since she first saw him erect, but she wouldn't be admitting that. Long and thick, it was the head of his staff that was the most impressive part. She covered the entire knob with her mouth, running her tongue around the rigid lip.

Enrique moaned as she sucked and licked and moved on him. The skin was like silk, and yet the flesh beneath was rock hard. He tasted slightly salty, too.

Enrique reached out and hauled her up to him, taking her mouth in a possessive kiss.

It looks like my time for control is done.

He flipped her over, hands greedily roaming her body. The pleasure was everywhere. Deep in her belly where his teasing fingers incited tingles of awareness. In the throb of her nipples as his mouth suckled on her.

She gasped and grabbed his shoulders, needing an anchor in the storm he'd thrust her into.

Her eyes were closed, heat surging down her legs as he teased and tasted her. Her belly tightened, and she cried out. He moved, lining himself up before thrusting into her in one move, sheathing himself to the hilt with a loud moan.

Sarah cried out at the welcome invasion, pleasure soaring inside of her at his possession.

Enrique cursed and slowly withdrew. Sarah's eyes flew open, not understanding why he'd left her.

"Turn over," Enrique motioned to her.

He wanted her to flip?

Okay...

She rolled over slowly and lay on her stomach, looking back at him over should. She wanted to turn the light off, or something. This was not her best view.

"God, you're beautiful," Enrique said, surprising her. He sounded like he meant it, too.

He knelt on the bed behind her and tugged on her hips, bringing her up so that she was on her knees. Before she could feel self–conscious he thrust straight into her ready body.

Sarah's head came back on a moan, this new position hitting all the right spots inside her.

Enrique ran his hands over her back and moved them around her front to cup her breasts. Then he began to move, a slow rhythmic dance. Straightening, he grasped her hips and dealt her clean, deep strokes that made her body clench with each thrust.

"Oh, God..." Sarah moaned, dropping her head, so she lay lower on the bed. She wanted him to keep doing exactly what he was doing.

Her pelvis seemed to tilt more in this position, and Enrique drove deeper. Sarah reached up with one hand and threaded her fingers through his where his hand held her hip.

He gripped her hand tightly and moved faster, pushing her higher and higher. She couldn't keep her eyes open, and her belly was tightening further and further. It wouldn't be long; she could feel the tendrils of her orgasm tickling at her insides.

Sarah gasped, holding her breath as the wave crashed into her. Heat flowed over her, making her shudder and shake, crying out a mere second before she heard Enrique follow her over into oblivion.

She collapsed onto her side, still breathing heavily. The room was too warm, and their skin was slick with sweat. But they lay in each other's arms, panting, and enjoying the intimacy of the aftermath of their passion.

As their breathing slowed and the silence began to tease her, Sarah, propped herself up on one elbow and stared down at her lover.

"So, tell me why you aren't married," Sarah asked him the inevitable question that had been plaguing her.

"Tell me why you were a virgin until last night." Enrique countered.

Sarah smiled at him. *No way.*

"You first."

Enrique untangled himself slightly and pushed himself onto his side, so they were now facing.

"I'm not married because I haven't met anyone I want to be married to. I'll marry when, and if, I want to. Not because I have to."

She cocked her head. That sounded far too simple.

"And kids? You don't want kids?"

He did a half shrug.

"I might. But they scare me. I have no idea what to do with Amalia, and I don't know what sort of father I'd make."

He turned onto his back and looked up at the ceiling.

Sarah sighed and reached for him. His body language told her he was trying to shut her out, but she wouldn't allow him to. In her mind, they had just shared in the most intimate thing you could do with another person, and now he wanted to hide from her?

No.

Laying her calf across his thigh and her arm across his chest, she cuddled into the nook of his neck.

"You would be whatever sort of father you wanted to be. You could be awesome if you wanted to be."

"Now you tell me," Enrique said, ignoring what she'd said. Repeating his initial movement, he pushed her off him again so they could lay facing each other.

Sarah sighed at his need for physical space, then remembered his question and blushed a little.

"I just never found anyone worth sleeping with."

"What do you mean by that?" Enrique asked, pushing her for a deeper response.

"Well…" Sarah swallowed, not quite sure how much to tell him. "I just didn't want to share my body with anyone before now. I've had boyfriends, but no one I ever wanted to sleep with."

"Until me?"

Enrique's question reverberated in the room. Wasn't the answer obvious?

"Until I met you. Yes."

Enrique groaned and reached for her. Kissing her breathless.

He reached for another condom, covered himself and pushed her onto her back. Sarah raised her knees on either side of his body and reached for him.

"I don't know how this is going to work, Sarah," Enrique admitted to her softly, stalling in his movements. "I don't want to hurt you."

His eyes opened for her, and Sarah saw the pain, the worry.

She hurried to reassure him. She wasn't sure how this was going to work long term either, but all her common sense was forcing her to live the dream while she could. The future and the pain, she was sure, would come soon enough.

Wrapping her hands around his penis, she drew him to her entrance.

"You won't," she soothed him.

Enrique didn't need much convincing. He pushed into her gently, filling her, stretching her. Sarah's head fell back as unshed tears lubricated her eyes.

Enrique buried his head in her neck, pushing them both higher and higher as he increased the speed of his thrusts. He ducked his mouth and drew on one of her nipples. Sarah gasped as the pleasure built and then crashed over her. She shuddered and whispered his name into the night.

Chapter Eight

The next three weeks passed like a dream for Sarah. Each day she spent with a little girl she loved. A little girl who was learning Spanish at a rate of knots, which was funny and smart. Who needed cuddles more than any other child Sarah had looked after.

To say she was in love with Amalia would be an understatement.

She saw Enrique at 6 pm with Amalia, where he always treated her with the due respect of his niece's nanny.

Calling her Miss Louis almost always made her giggle, but she held it back.

After 8 pm she was Sarah, his lover. He treated her with all the respect and love that she could ask for. Some nights they sat in the dining room talking for hours, others she had barely eaten her dessert, and he was whisking her upstairs for a passionate lovemaking session. His appetite was insatiable, and some days she went down for a nap with Amalia in the afternoon because Enrique had allowed her only a few hours sleep the night before.

Sarah found herself falling more in love with Enrique as each day passed.

Her period was a week over due, and she was ignoring it. Convinced it was just late, she allowed herself to be fooled. When

Sarah started to feel sick in the mornings and the fatigue dragging at her couldn't be put down to a simple lack of sleep, she made a doctor's appointment.

She left the doctor's office with information on her pregnancy and prenatal vitamins.

She couldn't believe it. They had only made love once without protection, but that was obviously enough to conceive a child. What was she was going to do?

A baby. Her baby.

She'd have her own family again.

Tears slid down her cheeks and tickled at her nose. It had been so long since she'd belonged anywhere, or to anyone. This child would be everything to her.

But how would Enrique feel about it? He had made it very clear that he would not feel pressured into marriage and Sarah would not see him trapped. They did not have a conventional relationship, but she felt that given time, it could become one. Time she didn't have. She was six weeks along. She would have to find out how he felt about her and fast.

Enrique was leaving on a business trip to London, and she knew that tonight would be one of the last times she would get to speak to him face to face for a few weeks.

She hid the proof in her room and went about getting ready for dinner. She pulled out a new green top and a pair black pants for dinner that had been hanging mysteriously in her wardrobe and sighed.

She had bought quite a few pieces of clothing for herself from the small boutique in the village, but lately, clothes had started appearing in her wardrobe that she hadn't bought. Beautiful clothes that Enrique had ordered from the same boutique. She somehow knew he'd find a way around her refusal for him to buy her new clothes. The clothes were always elegant and the right size.

Did he have a preference or did the sales assistant choose everything?

She made her way to the dining room, her excitement and happiness bubbling inside her.

"Good evening."

Enrique turned to her, scowling slightly.

"Can you believe they're sending out Christmas fundraiser invitations already?"

Enrique threw the offending invitation onto a nearby table.

"It's only August!"

Sarah laughed. Hardly something to be upset about.

"Is that what you do for Christmas every year? Go to fundraisers?" She lifted an eyebrow.

Enrique shrugged. "We donate money, go to fundraisers, all that stuff."

"No, I mean for Christmas Day."

Enrique's eyes widened, and Sarah smiled encouragingly. He was often unwilling to share personal information, but she always got it out of him eventually.

"No, Christmas I usually just got out for lunch with my parents, if we are in the same city at the time. Otherwise, it's just another day."

Sarah felt her eyes widen in shock. *Was he kidding?*

"You're joking."

"No, why? What do you do?"

"Well, for the weeks leading up to Christmas I am usually decorating the house from top to bottom, depending on what my current boss allows me to do. I love having a huge tree but make sure most of the decorations are made by my charge. So, we do painting, popcorn threading, and clay baking for days. And then I bake."

Enrique swallowed loudly. "Bake?"

"Yes, cookies, gingerbread, chocolates, fruit cake, everything. And Christmas Day we always have a huge present opening breakfast feast and then a late lunch where we just eat and talk and sometimes sing Christmas songs."

Sarah broke into a huge smile while she relived the last few Christmases she had. She had been very blessed over the last few years with her adoptive families.

Enrique cleared his throat loudly. "Wow, I see you found my gifts."

"Thank you so much, Enrique, I love them." Sarah twirled around to show him how the new outfit looked.

Enrique wolf whistled softly, giving her an appreciative smile.

"I told you green was your color."

Touching his lips softly to hers he quickly stepped back from her. It had been his rule that there be no public displays of affection, but occasionally he broke his own rule. It was a good sign.

"I heard you went to the doctors today?"

Did he know everything?

Um.. say something normal.

"Yes, I've been feeling a little sick in the stomach."

"And, what did they say?" Enrique asked.

"Just a tummy bug. I'll be good as new soon," Sarah smiled despite the white lie. She couldn't tell him her secret yet. She didn't want to lose what they had right now, and she certainly didn't want him trying to 'fix' it.

She had decided this afternoon that she was keeping the baby and he wouldn't be strong arming her out of the decision. No matter what, she'd make it work.

If that meant moving back to Australia and altering her job and life forever, she would. She would have to. She wasn't losing her baby. They were her only living family and the only connection she would have to the man she loved.

"I'm starving." Enrique's voice broke into her thoughts as he walked towards the dinner table.

He pulled out her chair for her and then sat down in the opposite place.

"Cab Sauv?" He asked her, already moving to fill her glass.

"Ah, no thank you," Sarah said quickly, afraid her face would give her away she dropped her eyes to the dinner in front of her.

"No?" Enrique repeated.

"The doctor said not to drink for a couple of weeks. Just to give my stomach a break," she lied. Although it wasn't an entire lie, it was true the doctor had told her not to drink.

"No problem," Enrique answered cheerily pouring her a glass of water and himself some wine. He chatted about his work throughout most of the meal and during dessert he asked her about her day,

"So, how was Amalia today?" Enrique asked conversationally.

"Beautiful as always," Sarah sighed. "I read to her, and we did our Spanish lesson together with the new tutor. We went running and of course did our swimming lesson. The funniest thing today was when she told me that I must love her and when I asked her why she said, 'because you're all shiny.' I've never laughed so hard." Sarah giggled again aloud, reliving the moment this afternoon when Amalia had shown more insight into her heart than most adults had ever done.

"You do look healthy at the moment, Sarah. I must assume of course that I have something to do with that." Enrique added smugly, a smirk lifting his thick lips.

Sarah laughed again wholeheartedly.

"You would think that, wouldn't you?" She told him, chuckling at the indignant look on his face after her reply.

"It is partly you," she grew serious now, thinking that it was about time to lay her cards on the table. She probably wouldn't get a better opportunity.

"I do love it here. I love being with Amalia; I love this house, and of course, I love spending all my evenings with you."

"And nights," Enrique corrected her, choking the words out.

"Yes, and the nights, of course… Enrique, I hate to bring this up so early in this, uh, relationship," Sarah could hear her heart beating in her ears and had to stop to swallow.

Maybe she should wait another few weeks? She could probably hide her morning sickness, and she wouldn't be showing for a while.

No. She needed time to prepare to leave, and there was the little thing of her two-year contract as well.

"I need to ask you…. how do you… feel about me?"

Enrique just stared at her for a long moment, too long. "I enjoy spending time with you Sarah, but I don't know exactly how you want me to answer that question."

His tone was kind but flat.

Her heart ached, and her stomach lurched. This was the end.

Sarah knew he was trying, to be honest, but he was evasive as well. He knew exactly what she wanted to know. Sarah gathered together her courage and plowed forward.

"Look, Enrique; it's quite simple. I know that you said that all you could offer me was what we have in bed and I appreciate your honesty about that."

Enrique nodded but said nothing else.

"But I'm just not too sure how much longer I can go on without knowing how you feel about me."

There, she had said what she needed to say. Well, almost all of it.

Sarah noticed his silence and knew it was now or never. She would tell him how she felt or die trying.

"Because, I think I am falling in love with you."

There, now she had said it all.

Too bad he looked as though he wanted to crawl under the table and stay there. Sarah held fast; her chin lifted high in the air she waited for a response.

"Sarah, I, don't know what to say."

That about says it all, really.

"Just tell me how you feel, and we can move on. Please," she begged, her heart breaking with his obvious inability to return her sentiment. He was looking as scared as she felt.

"Sarah, I… honestly don't know how I feel about you. I enjoy spending time with you. You are an amazing woman who is beautiful, intelligent, and kind."

Sarah's heart sank, talk about letting her down nicely.

"You are so different than any other person I have ever met. I don't know if you and I would work in the real world."

The real world? What do you call this?

Her temper began to stir. After everything they had shared, he was going to patronize her.

"Stop Enrique; that's enough. I appreciate the compliments, but your true feelings are clear. I think we should enjoy tonight together, and tomorrow say goodbye to this relationship we are having."

"You're calling it off?" Enrique repeated, his mouth dropping open.

"I think its best. Don't you?" Sarah lifted her chin. Her heart was pleading with him to take her in his arms and profess his undying love.

But from the frown and the coldness she could see in his eyes, it was pretty obvious that wasn't going to happen.

"I suppose you're right, Sarah. Well then..." Enrique started, his usual confidence and bravado absent. He looked around, and her heart tugged at her to help him.

He was apparently shocked by what she'd said, but it hurt to know that he couldn't bring himself to love her the way she loved him.

She was worth it. She knew she was. But she couldn't make him feel the way she did.

"I would like you to do me one favor before this ends," Sarah whispered, standing up and walking over to grab his hand. If she only had one more night with him, then she wanted to remember it forever. "Show me your bedroom."

Enrique looked at her with a slightly stunned expression. His mouth was open and his eyes were wide. Sarah's chest ached with each breath.

This was so hard. He hadn't done anything wrong, so how to make him understand that she had to end it?

INSTEAD OF ARGUING with her Enrique chose instead to lead her to his bed.

They made love passionately, each so desperate not to forget any detail they repeated every caress three times. And at last, as they climaxed together, a tear slid unheeded down Enrique's cheek when Sarah whispered in his ear, "God, how I love you."

The next morning it was Enrique that woke up alone after falling asleep with Sarah in his arms. After they'd made love and she'd fallen asleep in the past, he'd always enjoyed getting dressed while watching her sleep. Her hair sprawled wildly across the pillows and her angelic face looking so innocent he could have taken a photo if he'd possessed a camera, she was that beautiful.

But laying here alone left a horrible feeling in the pit of his stomach. Was this how Sarah felt in the mornings when he left her? Regretfully he remembered her last words to him last night.

God... I love you.

They still hung in the air, thick and desperate. He had poured his heart and soul into their lovemaking without knowing it because this morning he was without those essential parts of himself.

"Oh, God," Enrique ran his hand through his hair.

What had he done? Had he fallen in love with the nanny?

No, impossible. He, Enrique Martinez, didn't fall in love.

He could hear his friends laughing at him. It would be obvious she hadn't been a conscious choice.

Sarah would never fit into his world, and they would never accept her. He was a firm believer in not crossing over, and the worst thing you could do was marry a servant.

He jumped out of bed, determined to reclaim whatever had been lost last night. Sarah had decided at dinner that it was the end of them, and despite his resistance to the relationship ending earlier than he'd like, he'd respect her choice.

That's what rankles you, isn't it? It was her choice, not yours. When has that ever happened before?

Enrique shook his head clear of the thoughts and quickly checked the bag Riccardo had packed for him to take to London. But instead of feeling energized and excited, he was lost, with no idea which way to turn.

Enrique searched for Amalia and her beautiful nanny before leaving. He stood in the doorway to Amalia's room and quietly observed the image before him.

A huge lump accumulated in his throat at the sight. They looked just like mother and daughter. Amalia was sitting at her dressing table looking happy and relaxed, Sarah standing behind her brushing the knots out of the long brown hair that was growing past her shoulders. He couldn't speak past the knot in his chest.

"Tio Enrique," Amalia cried, racing over to him.

She threw her tiny arms around his legs and hugged him tightly.

It was the first time Amalia had touched him without encouragement, and he looked at Sarah, not knowing what to do.

Sarah motioned to him, 'pick her up', and Enrique bent down and scooped Amalia into his arms.

She squealed with delight and wrapped her arms around his neck.

His heart burst, then rebuilt itself even bigger.

"I've come to say goodbye to you both," Enrique announced, handing Amalia over to Sarah.

"Okay," Amalia said sadly, her little face downtrodden now.

"But I'll miss you," Enrique told his niece, his eyes resting on Sarah.

"Me too," Amalia sang, giggling at her uncle, and struggling to be put down. She was an amazingly happy child now that Sarah had worked her magic.

"Have a safe flight, Mr. Martinez," Sarah told him, gently putting Amalia down.

He made no move to kiss her, and she made no move to reach for him. Something seemed very final about this goodbye, but Enrique brushed off the nagging feeling that he wouldn't see Sarah again.

"See you in a couple of weeks," he told them both.

Sarah didn't reply but instead smiled and squeezed Amalia to her side.

"Bye," they chorused together, Amalia's arms waving wildly as Enrique left the room and the country.

Chapter Nine

Sarah knew she had to leave Enrique's house as soon as she could. She had two weeks to find a replacement before he came back. She could feel the changes in her body already, but thankfully, no one else could see them.

She interviewed several Spanish nannies with the help of Riccardo and ended up choosing a nanny from London. She was slightly older than Sarah and had the same sort of experience.

Sarah explained to the girl, Rachael, that she would be on a four-week probationary period when Enrique got back, just in case he didn't like her. Sarah had to elicit the help of Simone to book airport flights for the interviews and Enrique's assistant was extremely helpful.

She didn't tell Simone the whole story, but she seemed to sense Sarah's distress and supported her decisions, meanwhile swearing not to tell Enrique until he arrived back from London.

Sarah had already dealt with Amalia's devastation.

"Why are you leaving me?" She had cried. Sarah had said that her family and friends missed her so much that she needed to go back. Amalia wasn't happy about it, but after spending a few days with Rachael, she was warming up to the idea.

Enrique hadn't called once. It was nearing the end of the two-week period, and Sarah wanted to book her flight home.

After many sleepless hours and arguments inside her head, she decided to ring him herself. He deserved to know that she was leaving, although she was still unsure of whether to tell him about the pregnancy or not.

Her morals said that he deserved to know, as all men did. But if she did, what would happen afterward? Would he demand an abortion? Or fight her for full custody? He was a wealthy, stubborn man, and she had no idea how this information would affect him.

She dialed the hotel he was staying at, then got connected to his room. She exhaled slowly, her breath hitching in her throat. It had been so long since she had heard his voice, heat curled in her pelvis in anticipation.

"Hello?" Answered a female voice.

"Uh, hello," Sarah stammered. "Could I speak to Enrique Martinez, please?"

"No, I'm sorry he's unavailable. Who's calling?"

Sarah was stuck, she didn't want to leave a message, but she also wanted to know who the woman on the other end of the line was. And then she remembered the voice.

"Valentina?" Sarah gasped. What was she doing in Enrique's room?

"Yes, who is this?" Valentina's snooty voice rose a few shrill degrees.

"It's Sarah Louis, Amalia's nanny."

"Ohh," came the bored response. "I hope you're keeping that kid under control because I'll be mistress of that house soon enough and I don't want some child ruining my life."

What? No... he wouldn't.

She opened her mouth, but nothing would come out.

Enrique didn't want that woman; he'd told her as much.

He wouldn't do that to Amalia... surely?

She tried again, but she couldn't speak. The shock had her arms and legs frozen.

It was only when she heard Enrique enter the room on the other end of the line did her senses become alerted again.

"Who's that?" Sarah heard Enrique ask.

"Oh, nobody, it's just the nanny," Valentina said just before the phone was dropped into its cradle with a loud bang.

Sarah stared at the phone receiver for a full two minutes.

Enrique didn't want her anymore; he wanted Valentina.

The realization took a little while to sink in.

Sarah hung the phone up and picked it up again just as fast. She dialed the airport and booked herself on the first available flight back to Melbourne.

Enrique rung back twice that night, but Sarah had refused to speak to him. There was only one answer for why Valentina had been in his room, and Sarah knew only too well. She didn't want to hear his excuses.

And you broke it off with him. You have no claim over him.

"Argh."

Sarah rubbed her stomach reassuringly and tried to talk herself into being calm. It was true. She had no reason to be mad. But every cell in her body vibrated with anger and betrayal. How could he? And so soon after they'd been together?

She heard someone cough behind her and turned around.

"I really don't think you should leave so soon, Sarah."

It was Riccardo, his thick accent cutting through the cloud of despair surrounding Sarah.

"Oh, but I have to," Sarah wailed.

"No, you don't. Stay until Enrique has come home."

"No, I don't think so, Riccardo. Thank you for helping me while I've been here. You have been wonderful." A tear slid down Sarah's cheek. She would miss her life here. The people, the house, Amalia.

"You should stay, I know how much you care for Amalia, and for Enrique. They would be lost without you."

Sarah choked on a laugh. "Amalia loves Rachael already and as far as Enrique goes, well… I think he will do just fine without me."

"Sarah, Enrique cares about you a lot more than he would lead you to believe."

A sob broke out from Sarah's strangled, tight throat.

"I'm afraid he doesn't. He was with Valentina when I called tonight, and she told me she would soon be mistress of this house."

"Never," he whispered, his olive complexion paling.

"I'm afraid so," Sarah whispered back.

"Enrique does not love that woman. He would never marry her." Riccardo's tone was quite adamant.

"I don't think Enrique cares whether he loves her or not, he would see it as a good merging of their bloodlines."

Riccardo snorted.

"Sarah," Riccardo addressed her and came forward to hold her hand. "I have worked for Enrique's family since before he was born and I can tell you he has never looked at any other woman the way he looks at you."

Riccardo's words made Sarah gasp, her heart wanting that to be the truth so very badly.

Don't falter now. You're almost home.

"If that's true Riccardo, it doesn't seem to be enough."

With a sigh, she removed her hand from his and went to bed.

Sarah cried the whole night. Her last night in the bed that had changed her life. The bed Enrique had first made love to her, the bed they had made their baby. The bed he had taught her countless new things about her body and its pleasure.

The next day Sarah was up and had left the house before most of the staff had awoken. Kissing Amalia goodbye in her bed for the last time, she stepped into the limo and rode away from the Martinez manor, and Enrique.

ENRIQUE GOT BACK to his home the next evening. He couldn't have been happier to be away from London's drab weather and back to his beautiful Spain. He was looking forward to seeing Sarah, too.

He'd missed her.

And he didn't just miss the sex, although that was a definite highlight to their relationship and he couldn't wait to get her naked and under him again.

Instead, he found that he missed their dinners together, her company, her constant badgering at him for details about his life. Enrique didn't know what he wanted from her, but he knew he wanted to be around her and to have her around him. He was sure they could come to some sort of compromise.

As he walked into his home, something was different. He looked around the foyer. Something felt like it was missing. Enrique greeted Riccardo and noted his face looked uncomfortable. Odd. Not stopping to think about it, Enrique bounded up the stairs into Amalia's room.

Empty.

Noting the time, he realized that Amalia and Sarah would, of course, be swimming before dinner.

Enrique bounded down the stairs smiling and headed for the pool.

He stopped about ten meters from the pool and his smile turned upside down on his face.

The realization hit him like a cold shower. The woman in the water playing with Amalia was not Sarah. She was too blonde, too tanned, and had an unbelievably tiny body.

Exactly what you used to like.

A shudder shivered down his spine.

Not anymore.

"Tio Enrique," cried Amalia, struggling in the blonde girl's arms.

"Oh, Mr. Martinez, no one told me you were home yet," said the woman, climbing out of the pool.

"I'm sorry, but where's Sarah?" Was all Enrique could manage. His was head spinning a little; his brain felt fuzzy.

"Didn't you get her note? She left you one in your room I believe."

The girl smiled, towel drying her slim long legs in front of him. Enrique scowled at her obvious lack of propriety and the fact that she was drying herself when Amalia was still dripping wet.

Sarah would never have done such a thing.

"Tio Enrique," Amalia cried to him, lifting her arms to be picked up.

Enrique gladly scooped his niece up, not worrying that her wet body now stuck to his silk shirt.

"Amalia, where's Sarah?" He asked the almost three-year-old, hoping to finally get a straight answer from someone.

"She had to go home," Amalia stated sadly.

"Home?" Enrique parroted, not comprehending.

"Yeah, she missed her friends and her nanna and pa too much. She said goodbye to me this morning."

This morning?

She'd left this morning? How? Why? He'd tried to call last night, but the staff had said she wasn't feeling well. What had happened? Why had she left them? Left him?

He handed Amalia back to the blonde.

"I'm sorry, who are you?" Enrique straightened up, shaking off the confusion.

"I'm Rachael. I'm the new nanny."

"New nanny!" Enrique roared.

Rachael clung to Amalia and took a visible step back from his anger.

"I didn't hire a new nanny!"

What in the hell was going on?

"Yes, I know," Rachael explained softly. "Sarah wanted to wait until you got back from London to explain it all to you herself, but yesterday she changed her mind and flew out early. Some emergency she said. Sarah has asked me to do a trial period with you for a month and then let you decide what you'd like to do after that. If that's okay, I would like to do that still."

Smiling, she propped Amalia up on her hip.

Through the pain, Enrique saw that Amalia seemed to be happy and otherwise unfazed by this life altering change.

"Si. Alright," Enrique said slowly.

Remembering what she had first said to him, he asked, "You said she left me a letter?"

Rachael nodded, and Enrique ran off to the house.

He took the stairs two at a time, ignoring the telephone ringing and Riccardo calling his name.

He moved straight into Sarah's room to find it empty of all her possessions. She had cleaned it out and left it just the way she would have found it initially.

He hated it instantly.

That bed would have to be removed. The decorator would be called today.

Then he remembered the letter. Her letter.

Walking as calmly as possible into his room, Enrique found a photo and a handwritten letter in an envelope. The photo was of the two of them. Sarah had laid on his chest in bed and held the camera up over her head. He hadn't wanted the photo taken, but she'd teased and cajoled and begged, and finally he'd given in.

His heart broke in half at the sight. He looked so happy, and she looked so beautiful.

Enrique dropped the photo gently on to the bed and opened the letter, his heart beating faster now than it had when he had run up the stairs.

The letter read:

Dearest Enrique,

How do I tell you how I am feeling at the moment?

I am so confused and sad that I don't quite know how to tell you everything I need to say objectively. I have to go back to Australia. I love you so much that the idea of staying here watching you with other women tears my insides to shreds. Especially after Valentina told me of your plans to be together.

I always thought I could stay detached the way you do, but I just can't. I'm sorry. I know you can't change and I don't want you to.

You are beyond beautiful in every way. Thank you for everything you have shown me. The last two months have been so wonderful; I don't regret a thing.

Simone has my number if you have any questions, but otherwise Enrique, goodbye. Enjoy Amalia, I have done my best to bring her out of her shell, now all you have to do is love her– not hard, I know.

Sarah.

IT HIT HIM VERY, very slowly. Like slow motion bombs exploding, over and over again.

She was gone.

She had left him.

Enrique read the letter again slowly. She loved him, but she thought he wanted to be with Valentina? Of all the stupid things to think!

"Mr. Martinez. Simone rung to ask if you wanted to add a bonus to Sarah's final paycheck?"

Enrique heard Riccardo's words from the doorway and couldn't believe his ears. He had gone to London for two weeks, and the world had gone bananas!

"What do you mean do I want to give her any money? Why the hell did she leave?" Enrique demanded, shouting at the elderly gentleman.

Riccardo merely raised his eyebrows at Enrique's tone, and he calmed down. In the absence of his father, the man in front of him had often guided and helped him.

"Please, Riccardo, tell me what is happening here?"

"Sarah needed to go back to Australia, so she organized to interview new nannies, picked one then flew home."

Pardon me?

"What do you mean she flew home? How could she have just left like that? I have to call her and get her back here. Amalia is not going to cope without her. I'm sure her contract has stipulations about her resignation." He was rambling now as he pulled out his cell.

"Do you love her?" Riccardo asked Enrique abruptly.

Enrique stopped rambling and straightened his spine. "I don't see how that is any of your business."

"Enrique!" Came the curt Spanish reply. Riccardo hadn't called Enrique by his first name since he was five years old. He was a stickler for tradition. Hearing the old man who had raised him say his given name now stopped him in mid-stride.

"I don't know." He answered, dropping his head in shame.

"Well, take some advice from an old man. That girl loves you. But she is also too good for you to mess around with. Either you love her, and you go after her, or you leave her to get over you and find someone else."

Enrique prickled at the idea.

Someone else? No!

No one else was allowed to touch her skin, kiss her hair, and hold her through the dark hours of the night! He was her first; he should be her only. At least until he could work out what he wanted to do… oh, what a mess.

"Thank you, Riccardo," Enrique dismissed his oldest friend and employee.

Sarah did love him, but did he love her enough to sacrifice his life for her? He would have to change so much. His work would have to slow down, he'd have to travel less, he couldn't sleep with other women. It had been a long time since he had needed or wanted that freedom, he conceded, but it was losing that choice that was the issue.

Time was what Enrique needed and time he had.

He lay down on the bed and slowly fell into a deep sleep. A single thought was taunting him as he drifted off, he hadn't even kissed another woman when he had been in London. He hadn't even wanted to!

Chapter Ten

SᴀRᴀH ᴡᴀᴛ ᴛᴊᴏᴇᴅ; ʜᴇʀ ғᴇᴇᴛ ᴡᴇʀᴇ ᴀᴄʜᴊɴɢ, ᴀɴᴅ ʜᴇʀ ʙᴀᴄᴋ ᴡᴀᴛ ѕᴏʀᴇ.

Partly from her belly that protruded from her body, and partly because of the children she had picked up all day.

It was just over four months since she had left Spain, but it felt like four years. Sarah had fallen straight into a job with a daycare center that was working out beautifully. The hours were a regular 8–4pm or 9am–5pm, and she got to go home after work.

Home when she first moved back to Melbourne had been her best friend Tania's house.

A month later she found the perfect unit. Three bedrooms, one level and in a block of only two, on a nice street near her work. Sarah had the deposit saved but was worried about how she would support herself once the baby arrived. Her answer came in her final paycheck from Enrique. A HUGE bonus that was enough to put the down payment on the house was deposited into her account. Sarah had been shocked and sarcastically told herself it was for 'services rendered'. She'd almost sent it all back.

She had been a little nasty in her second trimester.

Instead, she used his money on the house for her and the baby, justifying that the 'whoring money' would be the only child support she would ever receive.

Their baby, Sarah smiled to herself, rubbing a reassuring hand over her swollen abdomen.

Her pregnancy had reached twenty-six weeks, and she could not be more excited to meet the baby she and Enrique had created together. Her friends had thought she was nuts not to tell the father, but Sarah kept her secret close to her chest.

No one was finding out the baby was Enrique's. She had gone over that particular fight with herself many times in the past four months. He had told her he would only marry when he wanted to. He wouldn't be trapped, and this pregnancy would trap him.

Sarah had too much pride to be married to a man who felt caged like an animal, against his will. He had made it clear how he felt, not only with his words but with his actions.

And to add insult to injury, he never called, not in all the four months she had been back in Australia. Not to yell at her, not to ask her any questions. There had been nothing. If he cared at all, he would have at least picked up the phone and called.

And although it was embarrassing to admit, she was still in love with Enrique. She kept newspaper clippings of him to show their baby and had secretly blown up the photo of them for her room.

She loved that picture; he looked so gorgeous, and she looked so in love.

It had been a horrible day when she had read about Valentina and Enrique being caught out for dinner in Paris. What they had been doing in Paris, Sarah could only imagine, and she did imagine. Every night she lay in her bed fantasizing about the man who had taken her virginity.

Exhausted from her long day and the baby growing inside of her, Sarah fell into a deep sleep.

―――――

ENRIQUE SAT at his dining room table and scowled down at the magazine in front of him. He never read gossip magazines, but this one had been left for him to read- with the appropriate page open and circled.

Only Riccardo would have the audacity to do it, and he secretly thanked the man for pointing it out to him. He had been no saint in the past, but the majority of the published articles on him had been mostly right.

This one wasn't.

There was a photo of him and Valentina at dinner in Paris looking quite cozy. The accompanying article suggested that they had been in a relationship for almost five months! If Sarah saw this rubbish she would be mortified.

Enrique caught himself thinking that way again and physically slapped his hand hard against his thigh.

Thinking about how the situation would influence 'that woman' as he called her, had become a full-time job.

Bringing his thoughts back to the problem at hand Enrique realized that the article was not only misleading, but it was also completely false. He had been having dinner with Valentina and her parents. However, the photographer had made a good job of making out that they were indeed very alone.

Enrique scowled again and tossed the offending magazine into the fire.

"I thought the same thing myself," came a familiar Spanish voice. It was Mateo.

Enrique laughed.

"Hello, amigo, what brings you here?" Enrique stood up to greet his friend with a hug and a kiss on each cheek.

"Just checking up on you. When I saw the article about you and Valentina I had to come by and make sure it wasn't true."

Enrique laughed again. "You should know I don't go after your sloppy seconds."

"And you are not totally insane." Mateo finished for him.

"True."

Valentina was neurotic, spoiled, and not in any way wife material.

"You look like crap, what's been happening?" Mateo asked, sitting down and facing Enrique.

"Thanks," he answered sarcastically. How did his friend know him so well?

"Talk," Mateo commanded, interlacing his fingers over his chest and leaning back in his chair.

"I don't know what you want me to say. I think I need a holiday." Enrique lied.

"You? A holiday? Why?"

The last time he'd taken a non-working holiday was when he had finished university.

That was over ten years ago.

"I can't seem to get into work at the moment. I think I need a bit of time off."

He had been thinking the same thing for a little while now and hadn't been able to put it into words. He couldn't seem to rouse himself to care about his work. He had no appetite for women, and all he wanted to do was swim in the pool and think.

"Who is she then?" Mateo smiled smugly.

Enrique frowned and glanced away. He wanted to wipe that smile off his friend's face.

"What do you mean?"

"I didn't know you'd been seeing anyone."

"I'm not," Enrique told him, his anger dissipating as quickly as it had arisen.

"Well, all I know is that a woman is the only thing that can put a look on a man's face like that. Not that I've ever seen it on your face before, but you know, miracles happen. Unless... there's nothing wrong with Amalia is there?"

"No, Amalia's great, she's never been better," Enrique told him quietly, looking down at his hands.

"That gorgeous woman still doing a good job then?" Mateo asked.

Enrique's eyes narrowed. "Yes, she is, but it's not Sarah anymore, her name's Rachael."

"Where's Sarah gone?" Mateo asked casually.

"Oh? Her? She left about four months ago." Enrique answered, striving for a dismissive tone but instead, his voice sounded shrill.

"Why'd she leave, then? I thought you liked her?" Mateo asked, sitting up straighter in his chair.

"Who said I liked her?"

"Oh, please. You have never been jealous of me in your life until I kissed that girl right under your nose. Don't you dare tell me you didn't care about her."

Mateo stared at him for a moment.

"It's her," Mateo breathed incredulously.

He was obviously doing a poor job of concealing the fact that it was Sarah's absence that was doing this to him. He should confide in his oldest friend.

"Yes," Enrique confessed, dropping his head into his hands.

"Well, what are you doing here with me? If you want her so much, go after her!" Mateo snapped at him.

Enrique's head came up. Did he just hear right? Had Mateo told him to go and get Sarah?

Oh, how I want to do that!

The life he'd thought he wanted no longer mattered, not without her in it. But what would his friends think about him marrying the 'help.' They would laugh in his face.

"I couldn't do that Mateo; you know that. What would people say?"

Mateo snorted. "People? When in the hell have you worried about people? So, she was Amalia's nanny. Good for you. You'll actually marry someone who wants to look after your children. Just look at this house. A month till Christmas and you wouldn't even know. Where's the tree? Where are the candles? You have a three-year-old to indulge."

"Amalia has her own tree." Enrique shrugged, not caring about such things.

"That's not the point. A woman like Sarah would decorate this house from top to bottom. She would light it up. She would make Christmas a day to look forward to, not just a day off work."

Enrique considered all this and looked around the sparse living room. Christmas was nothing to him.

Remembering the way Sarah decorated her room and the stories she'd told of her Christmas' in the past, he could see the life Mateo painted. A life full of love and warmth. With a woman who cared.

"But she has no money; she's a servant, Mateo!" Enrique let his greatest fears fly out of his mouth without thinking.

Mateo laughed, he laughed at him!

"Don't laugh at me," yelled Enrique, jumping to his feet.

"My friend, I'm sorry, but what were our grandfathers? We may have money now, but we didn't come from it. Not if you go back a few generations. If you want a marriage that survives the years like our grandparents had, I suggest you marry someone you can love and trust, not a spoilt, little rich bitch who'd think nothing of leaving you. Sarah would never do that. You could see it on her face when she looked at you."

"Now what are you talking about?" Enrique asked, hope sneaking into his heart like a thief in the night.

He blinked a few times, a strange dizziness consuming his mind. His brain was absorbing all the information Mateo was throwing at him too quickly, and he couldn't see the wood for the trees at the moment.

Hang on... His friend approved of Sarah?

"Oh Enrique, you really do have it bad, don't you? I could see it the night you had your party. Why did you think I wanted to get to know her? I couldn't let my best friend fall in love with a woman I didn't approve of."

"But you took her outside, you kissed her!" he was sputtering now.

"I had to take her outside because the sight of you and Valentina together made her cry. And I kissed her because I have never met such a genuinely beautiful woman before. Her tears for you just made me want to hold her forever."

Mateo stopped then, his body language changing. He sat up, throwing his shoulders back and jutting out his chin.

Enrique sat down with a thump, slowly assimilating all the new information. Sarah loved him; Mateo thought she was beautiful and Enrique had let her go.

Well, that would be remedied immediately.

"I've got to pack, Mateo. I have a plane to catch." Enrique stood up to give his friend a hug and a kiss on each cheek.

"You better make me your best man at your wedding," Mateo called out as Enrique ran up the stairs to his room, calling for Riccardo on the way.

Chapter Eleven

Sarah knew her days of lifting two-year-old children were numbered as she lifted Michael onto her hip. With her tummy expanding every day she just couldn't pick up the kids the way she wanted to.

Sarah looked at her cell and saw a new voice mail. She listened to her message, and her heart began to pound in her chest. So loudly she could barely swallow for fear the organ would leap out of her chest.

It was Enrique! He was in Melbourne and wanted to meet her for dinner.

No way.

She couldn't see him! He couldn't see her in this condition because he'd want to know why she hadn't told him. Sarah started panicking, her breath whooshing in and out of her chest with startling speed.

If Enrique found out about the baby, he would feel obligated to look after her and it. He'd hate her forever for trapping him into looking after a baby he didn't want. With a woman he didn't want.

She pushed the panic aside and focused on the problem.

Breathe, just breathe.

She couldn't see him. If that meant she had to avoid him, then she would.

Deleting the message, she went back to her work as though he had never called. Hopefully, he'd get back on a plane and go back to where he came from.

ENRIQUE HAD BEEN in Melbourne for a week, and he had called Sarah every single day. She didn't, or wouldn't, return his calls. He didn't know how to get in touch with her in any other way, other than hiring a private detective, and did he want to do that? What sort of stalker would that make him?

A thought struck him in the heart with a chunk of ice.

What if she's found somebody else?

"Mr. Martinez, I have found out where Miss Louis works," buzzed the intercom in his office.

Jumping three feet in the air, Enrique dove for the phone. "Please dial the number and get her for me."

Simone connected the call for him, and the phone began to ring.

His heart was beating so fast he could hardly hear the ring tone over the rush in his ears. It sounded just like the rush of the ocean in a shell, only ten times louder.

"May I speak to Sarah Louis, please?" He asked.

"Yes, I'll just get her for you," answered the young girl, covering the mouthpiece and calling loudly for Sarah to come to the phone.

"Hello?" came Sarah's beautiful voice through the earpiece.

The brightness of her voice rang through Enrique's body like the chime of church bells.

"Sarah, it's Enrique."

He heard her sharp intake of breath and heat infused his groin.

Damn, that woman has far too much power over me.

The slightest gasp and he couldn't wait to have her beneath him again.

"Are you still there?" He asked.

"Can I help you?" She asked, her tone frosty at best.

"Yes, you can Sarah, you can tell me how you are," Enrique spoke smoothly, hoping some of his legendary charm would win back the woman he wanted.

"I'm pretty good actually Enrique, how are you?"

"I miss you."

The words came out more desperate than Enrique was hoping for, but there they were, the three words he had wanted to tell her for four months.

"Enrique…" Sarah began, a clear warning in her voice.

Enrique started negotiating. "I want to see you. It's been too long. We need to catch up."

"Oh, I don't think so."

"Please, Sarah. I'm in Melbourne for a few weeks and would love to have dinner. To chat, like we use to." He missed everything about her, especially their dinners.

"I'm sorry Enrique, but we don't have anything to discuss."

Enrique clamped down on his anger. That was not the way to get through to her.

"Then I'll just have to come to you. Simone has the address of your new child care center, what time do you finish?"

Silence for a moment. Deathly silence.

"Well… I suppose we could meet up for dinner, maybe."

Yes! Her resistance is waning.

"Great, how's Friday for you?" Enrique asked.

"How 'bout we just start with coffee?" Sarah suggested. "Come over to my new place, and we can talk there."

Surprised by her suggestion but not adverse to it, he decided to agree with whatever she wanted. It didn't matter where they were, as long as he got to see her.

"That sounds great. Can I have the address?"

Sarah recited her address to him.

"Okay, see you at 8 pm."

She hung up, and he practically fist pumped the air.

So elated was he with the conversation with Sarah, he had the rest of the day off. He bought an engagement ring and booked them into a beautiful dessert place for Friday night. His proposal had to be absolutely perfect.

He wanted Sarah to be his wife more than anything else. More than he wanted his business to do well, more than he wanted to travel.

Nothing was worth anything to him without Sarah in his life. Gone were the days when he enjoyed dinners by himself and wild parties where he woke up next to some model he couldn't remember apart from the fact she was on some advertisement he'd seen.

Sarah's smile had haunted his dreams. He remembered her skin, her lips, and of course the amazing way she had developed in his arms over the magical month they had shared together. Despite her inexperience, she had pleased him more than any other woman ever had. She had been eager to learn and so responsive to his touch.

He smiled at the memory of the times she had come apart in his arms. There was nothing more gratifying than hearing Sarah moan and feel her spasm around him.

Enrique shook his head at the thought, trying to remove the images as he grew hard for the fifth time today.

Bloody woman.

He growled, then laughed out loud; she did have the most amazing influence on him.

On Friday night Enrique walked up to Sarah's front door and almost sat down on the step without knocking.

Fear and regret washed over him in alternating waves of hot and cold. What if she had found someone else? What if she didn't want him? His spine straightened in denial as his pride kicked at him with the strength of a mule.

Of course, she would want him, and if she didn't, he would take her straight to bed and make love to her until she agreed to everything he wanted. He grinned at the thought, giving him the confidence to knock.

A brunette with a worried look on her face opened the door.

"Hello, I'm looking for Sarah," Enrique greeted the woman.

"Yes, I know. I'm Tania, and Sarah is in the spa, she hurt her back today lifting one of the children. Do your best not to upset her." The woman frowned as she stared at the flowers he'd brought. "I'll put these in water," Tania told him, pulling the roses from his hands.

Woah.

The woman was certainly abrupt. He wasn't used to people speaking to him in that sort of tone.

But, if she was Sarah's best friend, as her protectiveness seemed to demonstrate, then he wasn't surprised she was so curt with him.

Taking a quick look at the unit, Enrique's chuckled to himself. Christmas had arrived. Sarah had the most spectacular tree he had ever seen, and she had covered every surface with decorations or tinsel.

Christmas paintings her children must have done were also stuck all over her fridge. *This is my future,* he thought.

"Sarah… I'm off, see you tomorrow," Tania called into a bedroom, walking out of the door with a stern look at Enrique. "Go in; she's waiting for you."

"Thank you."

Enrique held his breath and walked into Sarah's bedroom. The same quilt was on her bed that had occupied her room in Spain.

Enrique smiled as the memories came flooding back.

She can redecorate the whole house when we go home.

He walked into the bathroom with his throat tight, and his hands were trembling. He had been unable to prepare himself for the affect that seeing Sarah would have on him and when he finally saw her, neck deep in bubbly water, his heart leaped inside his chest.

Her bright eyes were staring at him, and his knees grew weak. A chair had been placed in the bathroom for him and he sunk into it gratefully.

"*Hola,* Enrique," Sarah greeted him in Spanish, giving him a smile that didn't quite reach her eyes.

"Hi, Sarah," Enrique breathed, his eyes drinking in her appearance.

"You've lost weight," Enrique noticed, unable to keep the thought in his head. She was paler, and thinner around the face.

Sarah smiled, "You have, too."

It was Enrique's turn to smile now. He had. He hadn't had the energy to do the weights required to maintain the size he was when Sarah had met him. He also didn't have the appetite.

"I hope you don't mind me having a bath. It's just been a long day, and my back's a little sore."

"No, of course not." Although the idea of Sarah being naked under all those bubbles was a hard image to keep out of his head.

"What happened to your back?"

"Lifted one of the kids at work badly. How's Amalia doing?"

"Oh, she's great. I've kept Rachael on as her nanny. Amalia absolutely adores her." Enrique answered honestly. He'd been surprised how well the English nanny had worked out, but then again, he should have known to trust Sarah's instincts.

Sarah smiled fondly, a light shining in her eyes as she glanced off to the side for a moment.

"How have you been? I see you've changed your lifestyle a bit." Enrique gestured to her new home.

That was what scared him the most. The changes she'd made. Why wasn't she with another family? Had she built a life here that he wouldn't be able to talk her out of?

Sarah laughed. "Yes. I decided if I wanted more of a social life and a family myself, I would have to stop working as a live-in nanny."

"And have you?" Enrique asked, fear in his heart.

"Have I what?" Sarah asked.

"Found someone to share this new life with?" Enrique held his breath, fear closing his windpipe like a giant hand wrapped his throat up in his fist.

"No, not at all."

Oh, thank God for that.

"How are you and Valentina?" Sarah asked, her tone strange and squeaky.

Enrique scoffed loudly. He had to fix whatever incorrect notions she had in her head.

"Me? And Valentina? There is no me and Valentina. Why would you think there was?" Enrique asked.

"Well for one, before I left, I rang your hotel, and she was there, and she told me she was going to be mistress of your house. And then I saw you two in a magazine together, so I just naturally assumed that she'd gotten her wish."

Enrique didn't know what to be more shocked over; the audacity of Valentina telling Sarah such a thing, or the fact that Sarah believed her.

"I wouldn't have Valentina if she was the last woman on the planet." Enrique spat. It was Sarah's turn to drop her jaw.

"But she was in your hotel room in London," Sarah persisted.

"She was there because I had arranged to have dinner with her parents that night and she came to pick me up. I've known Valentina for ten years, and if I had wanted her, I would have had her by now."

Enrique hoped Sarah heard the conviction in his voice and his expression.

She nodded slowly, and he took a deep breath.

He arranged the next sentence slowly in his head before speaking it aloud.

"And I know what I want now, and what I want… is you."

Sarah stared at him. Had she heard correctly?

"What did you just say?" She asked.

She sat up in the bath and leaned towards him.

Enrique moved across to the spa, kneeling in front of her and leaning against the tub. "What I want is you, if you'll have me?"

"Enrique, what the hell are you talking about?" Sarah demanded from him, raising her voice. Her heart couldn't take it if this were a joke.

"I made a mistake in Spain. I was stupid and foolish not to realize that you're the woman I want. I am so sorry that I didn't tell you how much I loved you when you told me."

Sarah just stared at him. She was dreaming, she had to be dreaming. This was the way her dreams always went. Things like this didn't happen in reality.

Sarah blinked, then blinked again, waiting to wake up. But she didn't, he was still there, in front of her, professing his love for her.

"So, what do you want Enrique?" Sarah croaked out.

"I want you to get out of this bath and let me take you into the city where we can discuss out future together."

"Our future?" Sarah's voice was barely a whisper. No words had ever sounded so sweet.

"If you can forgive me and if you still love me. I want to make a life with you, *mi amor.*"

Sarah buried her face in her hands and tried to control her breathing. When she looked up, he was still there, waiting for her response.

"Of course, I still love you…you big dumb man," Sarah exploded.

She had gone through hell the past four months, where had he been when she'd wanted him?

"Well get out of that tub woman so I can kiss you," Enrique demanded, jumping to his feet, and holding out his arms to her. He had never looked more beautiful.

"Uh, no."

Chapter Twelve

SARAH SWALLOWED HARD. HOW WAS SHE GOING TO TELL HIM HER news now?

"What do you mean... no?" Enrique asked, his eyebrows rising high on his forehead. Then he started to take his shirt off. "Would you like me to get in there with you?"

Yes, please...

Sarah had never seen such a devastating sight as the one in front of her. Enrique almost shirtless was enough to make a grown woman weep.

"No!" Sarah almost screamed the word.

Enrique's hands stilled on the buttons he was undoing.

"What's wrong, *mi amor*?" He asked, dropping to his knees in front of her again.

"I need to ask you something," Sarah told him steadily. She needed to get this out, and quickly, for he would know as soon as he touched her.

"Anything," Enrique vowed to her.

Sarah held her breath for a full minute and prayed for the response she wanted.

"I need to know if you want to have children with me."

Enrique smiled at her question. "*Querida,* that question will be answered when we have dessert."

The double innuendo made Sarah blush, and she felt her head swim with the new surge of endorphins he aroused in her. But that wasn't good enough.

"No, I'm sorry, Enrique, I need to know now."

His beautiful brown eyes clouded with worry. "Sarah, please. I'd prefer to talk about those sorts of things after we go to the city. I have a plan to fulfill."

Sarah held fast. She didn't care what plans he had. They wouldn't trump the plans she already had in motion.

"Enrique, I don't care about anything else, this is the only important thing. I need to know right now how you feel about having children with me."

She watched as her lover closed his eyes, then opened them again, the brown irises burning bright.

"Sarah, I can only hope that you would honor me with a child. You would be the most wonderful mother, and I would love nothing more than to have a baby with you."

Sarah choked on a laugh and tears began running down her face.

He could not have said anything more perfect to her. Even in her dreams, he had never been so eloquent.

"I suggest you stand up then," Sarah told him, smiling despite the tears that continued to flow.

"Why?" he asked slowly, but after she shot him a – *you're kidding me?* look, Enrique moved quickly to do as she had requested.

Sarah blew out a breath and swallowed the new tears down. Now was not the time for that.

She began to get up, pulling her legs underneath her carefully. She needed to explain and only hoped he wouldn't hate her for keeping such an important thing secret.

"I didn't want to tell you because I didn't want to make you feel trapped. I only wanted you if you wanted me."

She looked up at him. Enrique's confusion was obvious in his narrowed eyebrows and thin lips.

"I do want you, my beautiful one; that's what I've been trying to tell you," Enrique soothed.

Action was called for, so without another word Sarah slowly got up. The water sluiced down her body, the bubbles clinging to her breasts and bulging tummy.

"Dios mio," Enrique swore softly, his eyes roaming her exposed and expanded body. "You're pregnant?"

She nodded and held her breath, waiting for something to happen.

"Our baby? I can't believe it."

His eyes were as wide as saucers. "You didn't tell me."

Guilt swam through her belly, making her swallow hard. "Yes. I'm sorry. I was still feeling very rejected by you, and when you didn't call…"

His eyes widened and then he looked down coughing.

"So, would you have told me if I hadn't called?"

Her stomach dropped. Oh no. This was what she'd been afraid of. How could she be honest about this?

She reached for the towel she'd left on the basin and wrapped it around herself, covering up some of her nakedness. Even with the huge bath sheets she had, they didn't totally cover her now.

"I would have, at some point. I think. I don't know, to be honest."

He lifted his chin. "You don't think I deserved to know, Sarah?"

It was his tone more than anything that broke her heart. So soft, so hurt.

"Of course, I did. I just didn't want you staying with me because you had to. I assumed you were with Valentina and I just…couldn't cope. I'm sorry. Please forgive me."

Enrique stared at her for a long moment, then a slow smile began to creep over his face.

"You're the woman I love. There is nothing I can not forgive. Now, please, get out of that tub so that I may acquaint myself with my baby."

SARAH GIGGLED WITH EXCITEMENT, relief flooding her chest like a sudden storm. Hard and fast, soothing and hot.

Enrique helped her out of the tub carefully, wrapping his arms around her for a hug as soon as she was steady on her feet.

Sarah wrapped her arms around him tightly, made difficult with their child between them.

"You are the most beautiful woman I have ever seen," Enrique told her, his eyes glowing like embers, smoldering bright.

Before she had a chance to respond, Enrique's mouth swooped to catch hers in a heart-stopping kiss, as his hand came up and pressed against her belly. Their baby kicked, and Enrique broke the kiss to stare down at her stomach.

"Wow," he breathed.

"Come see my bedroom," Sarah dried herself with the towel, walking out of the en suite into her bedroom.

"So," She murmured against his lips, threading her fingers into his hair. "What did you want to talk about in the city tonight, before I totally wrecked your plans?"

Sarah saw Enrique's desire filled eyes clear and he pulled her arms from his neck.

"I'll be back in one moment."

He fled from the room but was back before she'd even put the towel back in the bathroom.

"Where did you go?" She asked. Then a thought hit her, and she rubbed her belly. "I don't think we need protection."

Enrique choked on his laugh and went down on one knee.

Sarah stopped smiling and stared down at him.

Surely not.

"Sarah, *mi amor*, I love you. Would you be my wife?"

Opening the velvet box he held in his hand, he showed her the beautiful platinum engagement ring.

Sarah didn't know if it was the hormones or her happiness, but she broke into hysterical sobs of joy.

"Sarah…"

"Of course, Yes, Yes, Yes!" Sarah yelled at him.

Enrique took the ring from the box and slid it onto her finger.

"I love you so much." He told Sarah again, this time against her lips as she pressed herself as tightly as she could against him.

Enrique pulled back and bent in half, a rush of Spanish coming from his mouth as his lips pressed against her belly.

Enrique straightened.

"Everything's all right with the baby? Have you been to see a specialist?"

Sarah spoke soothingly to answer his questions. "Everything is perfect. I've had two ultrasounds, and the doctors have been very happy. Do you want to see the photo?" Sarah asked, remembering the ultrasound picture she had in the dresser.

Enrique nodded, swallowing audibly.

Sarah took out the picture from the dresser.

"Here," Sarah said, handing it over.

Enrique stared at the black and white ultrasound photo, his Adam's apple bobbing up and down as he swallowed.

"Do you know what it is?" His voice choked.

"Yes," Sarah said quietly.

Enrique just looked at her, his eyes imploring her to tell him.

"We're having a little boy," She told him quietly. For the first time during her whole pregnancy, she was able to say the word 'we.'

Tingles of happiness danced along her spine.

"Oh, Sarah. We'll have our little boy and our little girl!" Remembering himself, he lowered his voice. "That's the other thing, Sarah. Are you happy to raise Amalia with me? I love her so much now, and I want to do what is right by my sister."

Sarah could not have been prouder of her lover. His tenderness and pride made him the perfect man for her.

"Enrique, I would love nothing more than to be a family with you, Amalia, and our new baby." Sarah raised her hand to cup Enrique's cheek, and she saw the glint of tears appear in his eyes.

Sarah squealed as the man who would be her husband maneuvered her onto the bed and laid her down. Shedding his own clothing quickly he lay beside her.

His lips trailed a path down her neck to her aching breasts, and

Sarah moaned loudly as his mouth tugged on one of her sensitive nipples.

She reached for him, running her fingers through his hair, holding him to her.

"I have missed you so much," Enrique moaned against her skin.

Sarah nodded, past speech.

"This has been the longest four months of my life," Enrique admitted.

"We've missed you, too," Sarah told him quietly, a single tear slipping down her cheek.

The 'we' obviously wasn't lost on Enrique as he moved down the swell of her belly, kissing each inch of her new expansion. Moving lower he put his head between her thighs and pressed her open.

"What are you doing?" she asked, sitting up and staring down at him.

"I'm loving you," Enrique persisted, pushing her back down so that she lay flat on the bed.

The first sweep of his tongue along her most sensitive flesh made Sarah sit bolt upright. His tongue swirled, nibbling, and feasting on her.

Sarah spiraled out of control at the speed of light. Heat swelled and tightened, burned, and burst in her belly. Along her thighs and up her spine. His touch ignited her everywhere.

Months of missing him caught up with her, and she clung to him as the most amazing orgasm of her life swept her up in its upward spiral. White light blinded her, and the blackness consumed her mind.

ENRIQUE HELD her while she shuddered, feeling the intensity of her orgasm through his mouth and hands.

He needed to get out his clothes, now. There were clinging to his heated skin and he wanted to be inside Sarah once again.

He jumped up and pulled off his shirt, pants, and shoes. Throwing them haphazardly across the room.

Sarah lay on the bed smiling with bliss, her arms coming up to welcome him back onto the bed.

He looked down at the bulge of her belly and had an idea.

He climbed back onto the bed and coaxed Sarah to lie on her side. He slid down the mattress and lay behind her, angling her pelvis back with his hands.

Hunger ate at him and he closed his eyes for one moment to get a hold on his control. When he was sure he'd last longer than the ten seconds his body wanted, his opened his eyes again.

He slid into her in one smooth stroke. Enrique moaned aloud and almost lost himself right then. The clasp of her body was so perfect… too perfect. She was so tight and wet for him that his body exploded with pleasure. Holding onto one of her hips and kissing the back of her neck he thrust into her, again and again, until she was crying out to him.

"My God, I have missed you so much!"

He was toppling over the edge of that incredible precipice, and after four months of missing the woman in his arms, he was in no mood to hold back. He increased the pace of his movements, feeling her stiffen and cry out as he flooded her with everything he was.

Finally giving her his heart, the only thing she had ever wanted from him.

Epilogue

Christmas Day

"Honey! I need you."

Enrique smiled from his study. Sarah rarely used the servants to convey a message, she just yelled for him.

"Si, mi amor?" He answered, stepping into the family room.

Amalia was surrounded by her unopened presents and was squealing with delight.

"Oh, good, you're here. It's present time."

Sarah pulled him into the closest chair and then dropped onto the floor beside Amalia.

"Tio Enrique first," Sarah reminded her former charge, handing Amalia a present.

Enrique's niece jumped up and handed the bundle to him. It was decorated in paper Amalia had drawn on herself.

He unwrapped the present with interest; he hadn't received a present in a very long time.

Inside was a silver star. It was one of those that sat on top of a Christmas tree. Enrique looked up; he hadn't even noticed that their tree was missing a star.

"This is for you to put on our tree every year from now on." Sarah smiled, rubbing her large belly with a contented smile on her beautiful face.

Enrique swallowed, a family tradition. Sarah was creating family traditions already.

"Of course."

Enrique was shocked to hear his voice break with emotion. He stood up, putting the paper carefully aside and gently placed the silver star at the top of the gorgeous tree.

He stepped back and examined it.

"What do you think Amalia?" he asked, lifting his niece up into his arms. An action that had once seemed so foreign and now appeared to be the easiest thing in the world.

Sarah stood up and came to stand next to him.

"I think it's perfect," she announced.

"It's very pretty," Amalia agreed.

"And next year our son will get to enjoy it, too," Enrique said, still a little nervous about saying those words. His life was too perfect. It didn't feel right to have everything.

Sarah smiled and grabbed his hand, placing it high on her belly. Beneath his palm his son rolled and kicked.

"I think he's enjoying Christmas already."

Enrique grinned, unable to contain himself. His house had been transformed and his life along with it.

This Christmas was only the start; he had a lifetime of moments like this to look forward to now. Thanks to finding Sarah, his life would be full of family, love, and beautiful Christmas days, forever.

The End

ARE YOU A FAN OF M/M contemporary romance? If you are – I've written some fun and sexy romances under my pen name Tamsin Baker.

Truth be told is FREE at all retailers and you can download it :
https://books2read.com/u/brGwXE

OR READ on for a sneak peek into that super steamy story!

TRUTH BE TOLD
PREVIEW

Chapter One

Picking someone up at a gay bar was not Patrick's ideal method of meeting new people, but it had been far *too long* for him.

Too long since he'd had the hot, smooth skin of a cock in his mouth. Too long since he'd felt the muscled body of another man against him.

He stood in a corner watching the men as they walked into the darkened, music filled room. To the left of him a group of blond men in their early twenties laughed and threw back Fluro-colored drinks. He lifted his beer and took another long swig.

Patrick lived in the middle of the city, a hive of activity that offered every person any sort of distraction they could ever want. Yet he'd hauled his ass out to the furthest corner of what was still considered *the suburbs*, hoping he wouldn't be recognized by anyone he knew.

He glanced back at the group of twinkies and considered one for a moment. He was young and thin, which wasn't all bad. He had pretty blue eyes and was wearing a tight black singlet.

He shook his head and let his hungry gaze wander once again. No, that's not what he was looking for. He was particular, that was his problem. One of his many problems.

Out of the corner of his eye he saw a man approach, sky blue shirt clinging to his broad chest.

"Hey, man, how are you? Can I buy you another drink?"

Patrick turned and his gaze crashed into eyes as bright as the blue shirt the guy wore. Wow. His cock stirred beneath the fly of his jeans and he found himself self-consciously swallowing.

"Yeah, sure." He chugged back the rest of his beer and followed the hunk back to the bar. The guy was of similar height and build as he, a hair over six feet and approximately two hundred pounds.

Maybe two twenty.

The gorgeous man smiled at him and that deep pull throbbed in his loins again.

"I'm Liam."

He nodded back. "Patrick."

He extended his hand and was thrilled when the hand that shook his was large, warm, and soft. Contractor's hands made him feel like he'd been exfoliated all over for days after.

Liam held two fingers up to the bar tender and grabbed the cold beverages when they were slid across the bar without any money, or words exchanged.

Strange.

"Wanna grab a seat?" Liam tilted his head towards the booths at the back.

Patrick nodded, saliva pooling in his mouth. This guy was more gorgeous than he'd first realized. Classic features, clean, smooth face, and ruffled brown hair that stood out in stark contrast to his bright blue eyes.

They slid into the booth and turned to look at each other.

"Been here before?" Liam asked him.

Classic pick-up line.

He shook his head, and almost moaned as Liam's hand slid over his knee. Presumptuous move, but hey, it was what he wanted. "You?"

Liam laughed and looked around the bar. "Yeah, I own it."

He choked on his beer. *He what?*

"You're kidding?"

Liam chuckled again. "Well, part owner. My uncle owns the other half. When we first set up he had the money and know-how to give me a hand."

Patrick looked around the bar with fresh eyes and now that he wasn't just scoping out the guys, he managed to notice the clean furniture, the good lighting, and the great music. Amazing how he hadn't seen that before.

"What do you do, Patrick?"

Liam's hand began to run up his thigh, and his cock throbbed, aching to be let out of its trap.

Patrick took a sip of his beer. What was the question again?

Oh, yeah... that's right. This was the chit-chat part. "I'm a lawyer in the city."

"Yeah? What sort of law?"

Liam's hand was now inches away from his cock, stroking his upper thigh. His magical fingers were lighting a fire of pleasure along Patrick's muscles.

Why were they talking work when all he wanted to do was bend Liam over and fuck the shit out of him? Heat flamed in his cheeks at the thought, and of the blazingly hot image in his mind.

"Ah..." He coughed to clear his mind from the gutter. "Commercial law, mostly."

Liam chuckled again, running his hand back down Patrick's thigh, away from where Patrick ached to feel it most.

"Where were you six months ago when I needed you? I so could have used your help when I was buying this place."

Patrick smiled, looking into the bluest eyes he had ever seen. Fuck, he wanted this guy.

"Can we get out of here?" he surprised himself by asking.

Liam's eyes grew hotter and they dropped to watch as Patrick ran his tongue over his lower lip, nervous as all hell.

"Right now?"

He nodded and grabbed Liam's hand, forcing it to the rock-hard erection he had beneath his denim.

Liam groaned and rubbed his hand over Patrick's aching balls.

"It's a Thursday night so I'd better let my uncle know I'm leaving. My place or yours?"

A moment of alarm seized him. He couldn't take Liam back to his place. "Your place, if it's closer. I live in the middle of the city."

And in the most homophobic building on the planet. No way could he take Liam home with him.

Liam smiled, withdrew his hand, and turned away. Patrick moved to slide out of the booth when Liam turned back to him, seeming to think better of leaving.

"Let's see, shall we?" Liam asked just before he moved closer.

Hot lips pressed against his and Patrick's eyes slid shut. This was what he had been missing!

Patrick moaned and slid his hands into Liam's hair, pulling him closer as Liam's big hands wrapped around his waist. His lips parted, welcoming the thrust of Liam's tongue, dueling and parrying with it, unable to keep back the sounds of desire bubbling in his mouth.

It went on and on, their hands grappling over each other's clothes in the tiny booth. When they finally drew back, it felt like they'd indulged in the longest make-out session ever, both of them panting heavily.

"My place," Liam grunted, sliding out of the booth and walking over to the bar like a cowboy.

Patrick chuckled. He liked to think he was the reason Liam now walked with a true western swagger.

Liam spoke a couple of words to the older man standing next to the bartender and grabbed the keys tossed across the counter.

Blue eyes turned on him and a shot of arousal coursed through his veins. The anticipation raised the air temperature around him to inferno level.

Liam flicked his head towards the door and Patrick got to his feet, his knees shaking slightly. He didn't think he'd ever been kissed like that. Not with such passion, or finesse.

They walked outside together, not touching, which was insanely hard to do. But Patrick was afraid that if he did reach out for Liam, they would be fucking in the car park within minutes.

"I live about two blocks from here, do you want to follow me in your car?"

He nodded, unable to form words. Liam's nipples were hard and pressing against the thin cotton of his shirt.

Fuck he's hot.

Liam opened the door of a nearby black RAV 4 as Patrick walked over to his black Merc and climbed inside. He turned the key in the ignition and followed Liam, his heart pumping a steady tattoo against his sternum the whole time.

They were there within minutes.

Patrick's hands shook as he turned the car off, stepped out, and shut the door. His stomach clenched in arousal and nerves. It had been so long since he'd done anything like this.

"Hey, Patrick," Liam called to him from the front porch of a small neat, brick home.

How quaint.

As they stepped through the front door though, he saw that there was nothing quaint about the interior of the house. There were black and white photos of naked men, artistically draped over furniture and motor bikes, on the walls.. A rainbow flag was displayed proudly inside the living room and yet, the furniture was all minimalist. Clean lines and basic colors.

Liam suddenly grabbed him by the shirt and tore, ripping the buttons off Patrick's top and pulling it from his body.

Turnabout's fair play. He grabbed Liam's blue shirt and ripped it the same way, using as much force as he could. The buttons popped off and the shirt gave way so that Patrick got his first glimpse of Liam's chest.

Patrick knew he was built well, having spent a lot of time at the gym during his adult years and he ate right. But Liam's body was so much better. Rock-hard and well proportioned, Liam had the chest, shoulders, and arms that any man would die to possess.

"You are so hot," Patrick couldn't help saying as he reached out and ran his hands over Liam's large pecs, tweaking both small nipples between his fingertips. It might be cliché, but it was the damn truth.

Liam moaned as though Patrick's touch lit him up on the inside. Then Liam grabbed him by the ass, hauling Patrick against his body.

"No, you're hot."

Liam kissed with a passion Patrick had never experienced before. His lips, strong and sure. Patrick wrapped his arms around Liam's big shoulders and gave everything he got. He nipped and licked, sucked and groaned.

Liam pulled back and reached for the button on Patrick's jeans. "Top or bottom?" he panted, pulling at the buttons and pushing the denim down Patrick's thighs.

Patrick's cock rose against gravity, throbbing in relief at being freed from its confines.

"You do both?" Patrick asked, surprised. He hadn't come across that very often in a man Liam's size.

Liam smiled as though he knew the answers to all the secrets of the universe, then knelt down to undo the laces on Patrick's shoes and pull his pants off his legs.

Patrick shivered—naked, and far too aroused.

"I prefer top, but I can." Liam stood up and pulled his own dress pants down his thighs, kicking off his shoes as he went.

He'd been commando.

The biggest dick Patrick had ever seen in real life sprang up, pointing directly at him. Delicious. Long and perfectly poised. The large head glistened with pre cum and made Patrick's heart pound with excitement.

Liam grinned, "But you know, I'd love to fuck your ass if you'd let me."

Patrick couldn't stop himself, he had to taste Liam's cock. He dropped to his knees and took the beautiful, big head into his mouth.

Fuck, he tastes good.

Patrick sucked hard, loving the feel of the hot skin against his tongue. He began to move up and down on Liam, faster. He tasted so sweet and the sensation of Liam's cock moving through his lips made his own cock pulse so hard.

Liam pushed a finger into his mouth and pulled him off, chuckling softly. "How long's it been for you?"

Heat rose in Patrick's cheeks, "A while, why? Was I that bad?" Embarrassment flooded him. How could he get something so basic, wrong?

Liam laughed and pulled him into his arms, rubbing his naked cock against Patrick's.

"No, you were just sucking me like a man dying of thirst. We've got all night. No need to hurry."

Liam took his hand and gently led him into a bedroom where black sheets and a red coverlet greeted him.

Sexier than he'd expected, but still tasteful.

Liam pulled back the heavy blanket and lay down on one side of the bed, his smile a pure invitation to lust. "Come, suck me again."

Patrick took a moment, just as Liam had recommended, and paused to take in the sights. Before him was a beautiful man and he wanted to enjoy it.

For a moment he tried to remember how he'd enjoyed the impersonal fucks he'd experienced in the past. In uncomfortable cars. In dirty clubs.

How could they compare to this? And their night had barely started.

Patrick crawled onto the huge bed and kissed Liam on the lips in thanks, before diving down and taking Liam's beautiful cock back into his mouth.

"Oh, fuck yeah. Perfect." Liam groaned as Patrick found a good rhythm, steadily sucking and licking the juicy flesh while squeezing the base of the shaft. He wrapped his hand tightly around it and began to feel the first tingles of fear. Liam was huge.

"Get up here so I can suck you too." Liam said, tugging on Patrick's hair.

A sixty-nine? Patrick let go Liam's cock and looked up. "I've never done that."

Liam stared at him for a minute then gestured with his hands. "Come lean over my face and let's see who comes first."

Challenge accepted.. Patrick couldn't help the grin that spread across his face. Horny as hell because he hadn't been sucked in months, he knew he wouldn't last long.

He turned around and swung his leg over Liam's head, who made happy noises in his throat.

"You've got a great cock," Liam said as his hand encircled Patrick's dick and squeezed.

Patrick moaned and bent forward, kissing the top of Liam's purple head. "Not as good as yours."

Patrick sucked as much of Liam's cock into his mouth as he could, groaning as hot lips encircled him and sucked hard in return. He could have come right then.

Moaning low in his throat, Patrick enjoyed his own pleasure for a moment before focusing on Liam. He sucked hard and moved his hand, trying to bring Liam closer to climax.

Every time he did something new, Liam mirrored him. If he pulled harder, so would Liam. If he deep throated, so would his lover.

When Liam pulled back to suck Patrick's aching balls into his mouth, he was gone. Heat raced up his spine and down his legs. There was no stopping it now.

He pulled his mouth off Liam's cock and cried out. "I'm coming, fuck… I'm coming." Patrick threw back his head and screamed when Liam's warm mouth enveloped him as he came. Wet heat rippled around his shaft as Liam swallowed the seed that burst from him in hot waves.

He shuddered and convulsed, pleasure vibrating along every nerve cell until he couldn't see for the lights flashing inside his head.

Then reality returned. Why had Liam done that for him?

"I win."

Patrick heard Liam's triumphant voice through the fog of his orgasm and could only moan in response and kiss his lover's cock again in gratitude. He had never been so overwhelmed.

"On your knees, Patrick," Liam ordered, bucking his hips to make him move.

Still groggy, Patrick crawled slowly off his lover's body and remained on all fours.

"I haven't bottomed for a long time," he said, though that was an understatement. Once, ten years ago, hardly counted. He moaned as Liam applied a liberal amount of lube to his puckered hole before pushing one long finger inside him. God that felt incredible.

Then Liam added another finger, stretching him. It hurt for a moment, and kind of burned, but Liam was gentle as he pushed more lube up Patrick's rectum.

"I can tell. Don't worry. We'll go slowly."

Liam knelt behind him, his big hands on Patrick's ass and legs. He pushed at Patrick's thighs and Patrick complied, spreading his legs wider.

Despite the fear creeping into his gut, Patrick knew that he did want this. Wanted this man's total possession. Wanted the deep ass massage he dreamt about late at night in his cold bed, alone.

"Are you going to come again for me, lover?" Liam asked as he reached around Patrick's body and gently pumped Patrick's cock.

Amazingly, Liam's touch caused his sated body to stir to life again. Patrick groaned. He couldn't possibly, could he?

"Looks like you can," Liam chuckled, pulling back to grip Patrick's hips. Liam pressed the head of his cock to his entrance and Patrick shivered. This was going to hurt.

He felt the touch of latex and let himself relax. Liam would make this good, he was sure of it.

"Thanks for the protection," he sighed, dropping his upper body down onto the bed. The bliss from his first orgasm still lingered, so he closed his eyes and let his whole body sink into happiness.

"Always." Liam grunted as he pushed the head of his cock into Patrick's ass. Fire burned around the rim as Liam thrust gently, feeding him a little more.

"You okay?" He asked and Patrick stretched his arms out in front of himself, willing his body to surrender.

"Yeah."

"Good. Then hold on." Liam pulled Patrick back and thrust most of his length into him in one movement.

"Fuuuccckkk," Patrick screamed as his huge lover pushed past the tight ring of muscles keeping him out and up into his body.

It burned so badly, but he loved it. He needed it. Total possession.

"You are so tight." Liam said, panting with the strain to hold still. Which he was, and Patrick was grateful for the reprieve to give his body time to relax into it.

The pain crested like a wave, then began to recede from whence it came. Patrick relaxed back into the mattress once again, letting out a sigh as he released the tension from his shoulders.

Liam must have felt it, the moment Patrick let go of the pain, because he began a slow thrust and retreat rhythm, finally burying his whole length inside.

Then he began to move faster, his cock easily sliding in and out of Patrick's body.

Patrick pushed up on his hands once again, enjoying the way Liam's balls slapped against his own. Patrick's cock swelled to full length. His belly quivered as his whole world centered around that one area of his body.

"You're huge," he managed to get out.

Liam laughed and pulled Patrick's cheeks further apart, making the glide easier. "You have the hottest ass. I could stay in you all night."

Patrick's face heated with a blush. He loved hearing Liam say that, because he wanted Liam to stay there too.

Patrick pushed back against his lover, meeting his thrusts with his own.

"Oh my God," he groaned as Liam's cock made blissful contact with his prostate, over and over again. Pleasure curled inside of him, making his hands clutch the sheets beneath him. God, he was going to come again. "Don't stop."

Liam grunted and picked up the pace, changing his angle slightly so he was hitting Patrick's prostate perfectly.

"Aaagghh." Screaming out his second, more intense orgasm as it ripped through him, Patrick's balls tightened to the breaking point and he shot cum all over the sheets beneath him.

Liam thrust a few more times, prolonging Patrick's orgasm, until he too shuddered and moaned.

Instead of pulling out quickly as Patrick expected, Liam bent over him and pressed his chest to Patrick's back. Big arms came down on either side of his shoulders and hot, slick skin touched his. Patrick couldn't help arching up into it as Liam pressed his lips to the back of his neck.

How strangely intimate a simple kiss could be, after completely sharing their bodies with each other. Liam slowly pushed back up again and gently pulled out, leaving Patrick feeling oddly alone.

Patrick groaned as his ass complained. Sore, utterly spent, and yet empty now that Liam was no longer inside him.

Liam moved away and wrapped up the condom, wiping himself clean with the tissues as he went.

"That was amazing."

Patrick fell forward onto his belly and rolled to look at his lover. Liam was a god of a man. His thighs were massive, his belly flat, and his cock huge, even when flaccid.

"You're telling me? I'm an orgasm ahead of you."

Liam chuckled as he picked up a small towel and threw it down onto the wet spot on the bed.

"Use that often?" Patrick asked without thinking, the coincidence of Liam having a towel lying there for such a use far too convenient.

He could have bitten off his own tongue as soon as the words left his mouth. He had no right to be jealous.

Liam climbed back onto his bed and lay down, grinning like the devil himself. Blue eyes lit up when he spoke. "Yeah, all the time. Why?"

Patrick blushed properly this time, his face aflame with heat. He wanted to leave and he had to fight the irrational feeling.

He shouldn't feel like he'd been used, after all, he was the one who'd been trawling the bar for a one-night stand tonight.

But some ridiculous part of him wanted this to be special between them. He experienced this sort of intimacy so infrequently that he never stopped to consider that other men had it all the time.

The sinking feeling wasn't going away, so it looked like his night had just run out of time.

"I'd better go," he said, turning to dress to leave. Why did it have to feel so shit when it was all said and done?

Liam's warm hand grabbed his arm and pulled him back so they were facing each other again.

"Why? You still owe me an orgasm," Liam said, those twinkling blue eyes still dancing.

Patrick smiled, but knew it didn't reach his eyes. He did owe Liam. Pity it had to feel like an exchange of services. So dirty.

"Now?" he asked, scanning Liam's lithe body. His dick was limp, lying across his thigh. Did he want a hand job, perhaps?

Liam jumped out of bed and turned the light off suddenly.

Patrick blinked several times, waiting for his eyes to readjust. The mattress dipped as Liam slid back onto it.

"In the morning," Liam's sleepy voice purred as he pulled Patrick in for a kiss.

Patrick couldn't possibly. Tomorrow was Friday. "I can't stay."

Liam pushed at Patrick's shoulders so he rolled away, then he got scooped up and pulled against Liam's hard chest. Heat enveloped him like a summertime breeze.

Fuck, it felt good.

"Call in sick. I'm sure you've got at least a day you can use."

Patrick's eyes slid shut as Liam's skillful hands stroked his chest and abs slowly.

"I could …" he heard himself say. Truth be told, he'd only used one sick day in the five years he'd worked at his firm.

Liam chuckled against his ear and whispered. "That towel is my cum towel for when I pull myself off at night, wishing for a man like you in my bed. It's been months for me too."

A warm flush spread over Patrick's whole body as the words registered and he smiled as he drifted asleep, clutching Liam's hand to his chest.